<u>DEDICATION</u>

To Stergios Zacharia, thank you for bringing my Beamer's smile back and showing us how a man treats a woman.

DISCLAIMER

This is a work of fiction. Names, characters, places, and incidents herein are products of the author's imagination or used fictitiously and are not to be assumed authentic or fact. Any resemblance to actual events, locations, organizations, or persons, living or dead, is purely coincidental.

Blackout
By
Cate Mckoy

Chapter 1

Sheriff Cade Myers strode along Main Street. He left his car at the sheriff's station. When he had an early morning shift, he preferred to park his car and walk Main Street, an old fashion beat cop habit. He was no longer a big-city homicide detective. He enjoyed the much slower pace of Eldred. Both he and the citizens benefited from his early morning patrol. He became familiar with early risers and their routines. And for them, they felt secure in knowing he was an active sheriff, not just a pencil pusher and an administrator.

Cade took in a deep breath of the crisp fall air. It was not cold yet, but there was a nip in the air. He loved fall. He looked down the line of seasonally decorated street lamps with big bright red bows and a string of multicolored lights running the space between posts, feeling nostalgia. The early Christmas lights didn't clash with the jack-o-lanterns at the base of the lampposts or the witches, ghosts, and goblins on business's doors and windows.

The time encompassing Halloween, Thanksgiving, Christmas, and New Year's Day was Cade's most favorite time of year. He loved the activities all the holidays entailed. This would be his second year spending the holidays in Eldred. As a picture of a beautiful woman came to mind, he smiled. Hopefully, he wouldn't be alone this holiday season like last year. He had spent last holiday season alone on duty as the newly arrived sheriff.

As he neared the bakery, old man Potter stood from retrieving the newspapers in front of his door. "Morning, Sheriff."

Cade smiled. Potter was insistent about having a hard copy of the newspaper. The Eldred Gazette was a dinosaur that put out a small morning edition of the local news. It had surprised Cade when he first got to Eldred. He hadn't known a single person back in the city that didn't get their news and information via the internet and social media.

"Morning, Clyde. How's Betty?" Cade asked after Potter's wife.

"Oh, you know her, forever a morning gal. She's in there setting out some new pastries." Potter turned to shout through the open door. "Betty, Cade's here."

There was a short silence, and then Betty appeared wearing her usual bright, bubbly smile and Halloween-themed apron, holding a basket with an assortment of muffins. "Oh, Cade, lovely to see you. How's Mary?"

Cade smirked. The old busy body wasn't just the best baker in a fifty-mile radius. She did double duty as the town's biggest gossip. "I believe Mary is just fine. Did you hear something otherwise?"

Betty started to say something, but Clyde gave her a gentle nudge. "Of course not, she was just asking after Mary. Betty, go on and give the sheriff his basket."

Betty's comely smile spread across her face, enhancing her rosy cheeks. Holding the basket of goodies aloft, she told him, "These are for you and your men. I've included some pumpkin spice ones for the season. Have a good day, Sheriff."

Cade tapped a finger to the brim of his hat and took the basket. "Thank you, Betty. Y'all have a good one."

The couple waved, and Cade continued down the street. He'd gone no more than two blocks when old Jeb called out from the doorway of the general store.

"Mornin' Sheriff. Fine sunrise, ain't it?"

Cade tapped the brim of his hat this time in greeting rather than a farewell. "Morning, Jeb. Yes, the sunrise was gorgeous. How's Susie doing today?"

"She's great, thanks to you. She was feeling scared stuck on the mountain road with a flat until you showed up and changed it for her."

"It's no problem. That's what I'm here for. Although, a young girl traveling alone should know how to change her tire and keep her cell phone charged."

Shaking his head, Jeb said, "I don't understand why she didn't have her charger with her. She's constantly on that thing."

Cade shook his head as if to say he didn't know either. "Kids today rarely think beyond the present. She'll be more careful now that she's had a little scare."

Jeb laughed. "I wish I could say you're probably right. Knowing my Susie, she'll forget her charger again, and I am pretty sure she didn't watch you change the tire, so she'd know how to do it next time."

Cade laughed. "You know your child well. She mostly stood off to the side and talked about the new store in the mall."

Jeb smiled. "That's about right." He pushed his ball cap off his head and peeked up at Cade. "How's Mary?"

Cade's eyes narrowed. "As far as I know, she's fine. Is there something you want to tell me, Jeb?"

Jeb turned fire-engine-red. "Uh, n-no. I was just asking after her. Y'all went out on that date, and I was just wonderin' is all."

Shaking his head, tapping his brim in good-bye, Cade said, "Mary is fine. Thanks for asking Jeb. Have a good one."

Cade continued until the very end of the main street, where the sheriff's station and jail were to the right. Across the street were twin four-story buildings which housed the municipal offices and courthouse.

On the remaining blocks to his office, he had been asked after Mary's welfare no less than six times, and the not-so-subtle hints about his date with Mary. He still wasn't used to the small-town grapevine.

Cade was a private man. He wasn't sure he liked everyone treating his first date with Mary like Saturday night at the movies. Although his dating Mary was new, his feelings for her were not.

Fourteen months ago, he had accepted the Sheriff's offer to the small Hamlet of Eldred, NY. He had been an NYPD homicide detective for ten years. He was burnt out. He needed a change. Losing his partner in a shootout after tracking a serial killer had been Cade's last straw. He put in for a transfer to another department. He'd been dating an ADA, Paula Shells. She suggested that a different department of the same 'machine' may not be a significant enough change. The minute she said it, Cade felt it to his marrow. It wouldn't be big enough. He needed to get away.

He had started his search for another position that night. The ad for an immediate position with the Sullivan County Sheriff's office called to him. He hadn't known the job was for *the* Sheriff until he arrived for his interview. The former sheriff had a massive coronary and died suddenly.

It turned out to be the change he needed. The small town was vastly different and also the same as big-city crime-fighting. Cade was just slipping into his groove a month after his arrival when he had found Mary.

He strode into the sheriff's office, and as soon as the door closed, the dispatcher-receptionist, Sally Fone, assailed him. He sighed, mentally preparing himself for an encounter with Sally. The woman was a character.

"Where ya been? Thangs are a-brewin'." Sally had a dramatic flair about her. Everything was either dead boring or DefCon One. There was never a middle setting with her.

Sighing, handing her the basket of muffins, Cade passed her. "Do you mind if I get to my office first?"

As he rounded the high reception desk, Sally trailed after him and passed the bullpen of the deputies' desks to his office. His ass hit his chair, and Sally began.

Putting the basket down on his desk and waving several pink message slips, she moved her bifocals from the top of her head to her eyes. "Let's see here, that fancy New York D.A. called to remind you of a case coming up that you're testifying in," She placed the slip on his desk. "An agent with the Marshal's Service called said he'd be here about eight." She put another slip on top of the first.

"What does the Marshal's Service want with Eldred and me?"

"Beats me. You'll find out at eight. Mr. Simmons called to let you know he's out of the hospital, and the specialist said there's no permanent damage to the nerves in his hand."

"Thank God!" Cade said with feeling. "I have to find this nuisance before he kills someone!"

As though Cade hadn't spoken, Sally placed the next slip on top of the rapidly growing stack and continued. "The mayor has approved you as one of the available bachelor's to be auctioned off at the Holiday Charity Dinner."

"Hey! I didn't request to be a bachelor!" Cade scowled in frustration.

Sally simply replied, "Yes, you did."

Shaking his head in confusion, "I did no—" Cade shut his mouth when he noticed the calculating gleam in Sally's bright blue eyes. "And why do I want to be a bachelor?"

"Because you want Mary to bid on you."

Cade smirked. It seemed the whole town knew about his interest in the beautiful librarian. There was one thing he *did* miss about the city, its anonymity. He had been looking forward to the much slower pace of this job and town. However, the gossip was annoying. Eldred had lived up to the small-town lore. The scenery was fantastic; it was quiet, low crime, and people left their doors unlocked. Everyone knew everyone else and minded everyone's business.

The Eldred community was a small mix of primarily white, few blacks, even fewer Hispanics, and a spattering of other ethnicities. It boasted impressive vistas, farmland, surrounding mountains, and narrow, winding roads. The unused-to-silence went a long way in helping Cade to relax. The city had *never* been quiet. The crime in the city was high. The crime rate in Eldred was low. It was almost non-existent, that is, until a couple of months ago.

A prankster was going around town wreaking havoc. The fool even left a calling card by marking the crime scenes with a painted red X. First was the stolen mascot, a goat of all things. The red mark had been left on the gate of the goat's pen. Then came the school bus tires' slashing with a red X garishly painted on each window of the bus. Due to the fact, there were only three buses for the entire town, and one of the buses had been in the shop for repairs, the school had been canceled. Then came the fire alarm pulled at the high school. The red X was left on an art classroom door, and the kids were sent home early while his deputies investigated. There hadn't been much to investigate. The school didn't have video like its more modern counterparts in the state. The paint had been left out in the open classroom where anyone could have painted the X. Since it wasn't a scheduled fire drill, the students had rushed the door before the teachers could get order. The lack of fingerprints on the paint can proved to be useless. There was no telling how many people handled the can in a public school. Forensics was not the way to go in this case. Eldred didn't have its own crime lab or CSU. If there were any forensics needed, it would be shipped to a state lab.

Cade assumed the prankster was just some dumb kid that didn't want to go to school or was bored and liked watching the school's activities disrupted. Up until two days ago, the pranks had been harmless. The school's principal, Frank Simmons, had nearly gotten his hand blown off with a cherry bomb when he went to check his mail. The red X had been left on the ground in front of the mailbox. Frank said he hadn't seen the X until he was on his ass, holding one hand in the other, experiencing the worst pain he had ever felt in his life. He was lucky. The damage could have been worse.

In Cade's mind, big city versus small town, the small town was winning. He liked being able to go home at night and having time to himself to pursue a hobby or, in this case, a woman.

"I can ask Mary out without putting myself on the auction block. Why is everyone in this town so interested in my love life?"

Sally smiled and proceeded to school him in the ways of a small town. "Come on, Sheriff! Everybody loves a love story, especially in a small town. And love being in on it from the beginning. Besides, yours and Mary's is a doozy. It's like one of those romance books my daughter reads. You guys are facinatin'."

Sally put her glasses back on the top of her head as she continued. "I mean, really, you're a new sheriff in town; young, single, good looking, great physique, and white. Mary is black, young, gorgeous, sweet as the day is long, kind, loves kids and animals." Sally paused for a dramatic effect. "And, holy shit, the girl doesn't remember a blessed thing about her life before you found her out cold, drenched on that dark road thirteen months ago. She woke up, and you're the first person she saw. She was hooked." Sally gave another pause to bat her eyelashes and give a dreamy sigh. "Ya gotta love that." Her smile turned teasing. "Besides, you guys sort of eat each other up with your eyes when you meet. Your voice goes about two octaves lower when you speak to her, and hers goes all breathy."

Cade regarded his dispatcher with a mixture of annoyance and affection. She reminded him of his mother, no tact or filter to speak of. Whatever was in her head came out of her mouth. "Sally, ever hear of tact and diplomacy?"

"Lying and deceitfulness? Yes, I've heard of them. Don't cotton to the ideas." Her glasses slipped down her forehead to her nose. "By the by, Mary called too," she placed another pink slip on the pile. "She got another one. This time on her back door."

"Damn it!" Cade swore. "Yet, another asshole I need to catch!"

"You mean nuisance." Sally corrected.

"No, I damn well don't. The prankster is a nuisance, but this guy harassing Mary is an asshole. A dangerous one. He is rapidly approaching a line which will have him crossing into felony territory."

Frowning, Sally suggested, "Do you think it could be someone from her past?"

Cade lifted and dropped his shoulders in confusion. "What past? She doesn't have one. I sent her prints to every federal, local, and private database I could think of put her picture in the local news outlets and surrounding counties, all to no avail. If it is someone from her past, why wait thirteen months to start this shit?" Cade shook his head. "No, it's someone she's met since being in Eldred."

"I find that hard to believe. Everyone adores her. They may not know who she was, but they sure as hell love who she is!"

Cade couldn't dispute that. Mary had a loving sweetness that drew people in. Her exceptional beauty first made her appear unapproachable. Her shy smile automatically put people at ease. It had certainly worked its magic on him.

He remembered the night he found her. He'd been on his way home and spotted a dark patch on the side of the road. The darkening sky was still light enough for him to see that whatever caused the patch was out of place. He'd parked his vehicle to investigate. After an entire month of nothing but paperwork and budget meetings, finding an unconscious female on the side of the road with head trauma had ramped up his adrenaline. He had called for an ambulance and waited at the hospital to hear the news about her condition from the doctor.

She had suffered a severe concussion, cracked ribs, and needed several stitches to close the wound at the back of her head. The extent of her trauma wasn't realized until she opened those beautiful brown eyes, looked deeply into his, and said, "Who are you? Wait—who am I?"

Considering the extensive search for her identity he conducted, Cade seriously doubted Mary's stalker was from her past. No, he was just creepy, leaving suggestive notes and gifts. Soon, Cade had to identify the stalker before the nut-job decided on a closer encounter with Mary. For now, he was keeping his distance.

Cade shrugged. "I can't think of anyone who doesn't like her either. Technically, we're not looking for someone who dislikes her. It's someone obsessed with her, imagining a relationship with her. He's dangerous! I'll get him!"

"I know you will, Sheriff." Sally supported. She turned to leave, adding, "Don't forget to call your fancy, smancy, New York City D.A."

Cade laughed at Sally's reversed snobbery, picking up the phone. Before he could dial, his morning deputy knocked on his open door. "Morning, Deputy Boyd." Cade replaced the receiver. "What's up?"

"Morning, Sheriff. I did a patrol of the high school and surrounding area before coming in, like you asked. All was quiet."

Nodding, Cade picked up the phone and dismissed Boyd. "Thanks; you can catch up on your paperwork and then resume normal patrol, adding an extra one around the school."

Boyd left, and Sally returned with a tall man dressed in a crisp business suit. His look and body language screamed, fed! Silently cursing, Cade hung up.

"Sheriff, this here is U.S. Marshal Zack Duncan. He needs to bend your ear."

Cade put on his civil servant smile and indicated his visitor's chair, glancing at his watch. It wasn't eight yet. Whatever the Marshal wanted was important. "What can I do for you, Marshal Duncan?"

"As you know, we run the Wit-Sec programs." At Cade's nod, he elaborated. "One of our witnesses was placed in your jurisdiction. You know her as Mandy Odessa."

"The elementary school teacher? She just took a personal leave of absence."

Duncan was instantly suspicious. "And how do you know that?"

Cade chuckled. It had taken him a while to get used to the small-town gossip mill. It worked better than AT&T. "Uh, I'm guessing you're not too familiar with small towns. You can sneeze at one end of town, and someone at the other end is handing you a tissue and saying 'God, bless you'."

"Well, perhaps this rumor mill can help us locate her. She missed two check-ins, and I've just been to her place. It looks deserted. We've intercepted chatter that the infamous hitman, Never-Miss, is headed this way to take care of her."

"I've heard about that guy when I was NYPD. There are an awful lot of murders attributed to him. He's like an urban legend. Is he for real?"

"The bodies he's left in his wake are real. This Never-Miss—can't believe adults actually dubbed him that— seems bigger than he is or otherworldly because no one has ever gotten a look at the guy. The most we have on him is a grainy photo at an airport. He's a man, not some ghost; therefore, he can be captured and sent to prison. Mandy Odessa's eye-witnessed account against the Dulca crime family is coming up in Chicago. It's imperative that I find her."

"Okay, Marshal. Why don't you make your way to my SUV outside, the one closest to the door, and we'll head over to the elementary school to see if we can find out where Mandy was headed. I just need to make a call."

Duncan left, and Cade successfully dialed Mary's cell phone number. Getting no answer, he dialed the public library. Again, getting no response, he hung up, thinking his small town took on traits of the big city he left behind. Checking his weapon on his hip, Cade made his way to his car. Worrying about Mary, he began ticking off the illegal activity that seemed to crop up overnight, a prankster, a stalker, a missing witness, and a possible hitman on the way. Small town living ...peaceful ...serene ...quiet...bullshit.

Chapter 2

Cade pulled into the elementary school just as classes were beginning. Marshal Duncan, following him, looked around with a shellshocked expression. "Is this it?"

Cade quirked a brow. "Didn't you see it when you placed Mandy Odessa here?"

Duncan shook his head. "No, her original handler left for maternity leave."

Nodding his understanding, Cade walked through the front door. Several feet past the entrance, he walked around the row of metal detectors.

"This tiny school has metal detectors?" Duncan laughed.

Cade slanted a brow. "It's *still New York* here."

"Point taken."

Cade led Duncan to the main office. He smiled at Lana Miles at the main desk. "Morning, Lana."

The woman's smile grew wide. "Hey, Sheriff Myers. How's Mary?"

Cade rolled his eyes. "Lana, this is an official visit."

"Principal Simmons is out on medical leave."

"I know. I am sure you can help me." Cade looked around, including the other two women in the office in the conversation with a smile.

"We'll do what we can. What do you need, Sheriff?"

"It's about Mandy Odessa. Did she tell any of you guys where she's headed for her leave?"

Lana shrugged and looked over her shoulder at the other women. "She didn't mention anything specific to me, and she would have."

One of the other women chimed in, "Mandy told me she was going to have a staycation, get some of her gardening done, and some indoor repairs and updates that she had been putting off."

Cade nodded and looked over at the Marshal. "Anything else?"

"Does Mandy have a boyfriend?"

"She's been dating Billy Tillman," Lana informed.

"Okay, ladies, thank you. Have a good one." Cade tapped the brim of his hat before leaving.

On the way to the car, Marshal Duncan asked, "You know this Tillman?"

"Yeah, he's the new recruit over at the firehouse."

It was a short ride to the Eldred firehouse. Cade's SUV took the last parking place.

"Wow, this place is full. This little town isn't so little." Duncan's surprise laced his words.

Getting out of the car and entering the one open bay, Cade answered, "This is a Sullivan County fire station, not just for Eldred. These guys respond to fires all over the county. If it were just for Eldred, we'd hardly need these many firemen."

"Hey, Sheriff Myers. What's up?" Lt. Tim Mendelson inquired, rolling from underneath the fire station's ambulance. He stood and pulled the cloth tucked inside his waistband, wiping his greasy hands.

"Hey, Tim. Is Billy here?"

Tim tipped his head behind him. "He's on mess duty today. He's cleaning up breakfast."

Cade made his way to the kitchen. Sure enough, Billy was knee-deep in soapy water. Cade's salutatory smile slipped when he noticed Matt Madson on the other side of the kitchen.

Cade stopped short of displaying his annoyance at the other man's presence. Matt Madson was his only serious competition for Mary. Other single men in town took a shine to Mary and wanted to get to know her intimately. But Matt was the only one near Cade's and Mary's age group that wasn't already married or in a relationship. Matt was also physically appealing in the traditional sense. He was charming, and the whole town considered him a good guy.

Until Mary came to their small hamlet, Cade had considered Matt one of his best friends. They hung out on their off-hours, watched sports, played b-ball. Because of the nature of their jobs, they saw each other often during their work.

Matt had been the paramedic that had responded when Cade called for an ambulance for Mary. The three had formed a friendship from that tense and unconventional meeting. It wasn't until after Mary was all healed and given a new identity so that she could earn a living and she had become settled into the community that Cade realized he was falling for the shy beauty. And, like had been his habit since they first became friends, Cade made the mistake of confiding in Matt.

Matt had then made his own feelings clear. He, too, was falling for Mary. Matt had taken his confessions a step further, stating he planned on asking Mary out, and he'd appreciate it if Cade respect his right to be with Mary more than his.

Cade had been shocked that Matt was bringing race into their friendship. From the moment they met, Matt being black and Cade being white hadn't even made a blip in their friendship. Being from one of the biggest, diverse melting pots in the world, Cade couldn't care less about someone's race. Their character is what mattered to him. He had thought Matt was of the same mind. Cade had been entirely thrown by Matt playing the race card.

After his shock abated, he became angry. What Matt was spouting about him being better for Mary simply because they both were black was the most ridiculous horseshit he'd ever heard. And Cade wasn't standing for it. Fuck that bullshit and to hell with Matt.

Even so, Cade had waited for Matt to ask Mary out first. They both were floored when she turned Matt down, albeit graciously. Confused, Cade had waited a full two weeks, watching while others had tried their luck asking out Eldred's beautiful librarian. She had turned them all down with a sweet smile. Exactly two weeks after Matt, Cade asked Mary out for himself, expecting to be rejected like Matt and the others had been.

Surprisingly, Mary had said yes. They had their first date on Saturday. He gave Mary a pause on Sunday so as not to smother her. A couple of the guys in town weren't taking no for an answer as graciously as Mary had given it. And she was being stalked by a supposedly secret admirer. So, after their successful date on Saturday, he wanted to give her space. Even though Cade had found himself aching to call her all day Sunday. Today was Monday. He had every intention of calling Mary and not letting go of their momentum from their great date.

From the look Matt was giving him, Cade could tell he was still very pissed. Mary had said yes to Cade and no to him.

Ignoring Matt's dirty look, he addressed Billy. "Hey, Billy, have you seen Mandy Odessa?"

Billy dried his hands off on his uniform pants. "I haven't seen her since Thursday." Taking in Cade's serious look and giving the man with him a curious glance, he asked, "Is there something wrong?"

Shaking his head, Cade spoke. "No, I just need to speak with her."

"Well, we have tentative plans to do the hiking trails on Wednesday and campout until Friday."

Cade and Marshal Duncan exchanged a look. Bringing his attention back to Billy, he added, "Tell her to give me a call when you see her. Unless you have an idea where she is right now."

Billy shook his head. "If she isn't home working on her garden, then I am not sure where she might be. My best guess is at the library. She and Mary are pretty good friends."

Cade nodded. "Okay, thanks. Don't forget to have her call when you see her."

"Sure thing, sheriff."

Cade and Duncan turned to go when Matt spoke. "Sheriff Myers, can I speak with you for a minute."

With a grim expression, Cade let Duncan know he'd meet him in the SUV. Then he and Matt exited the kitchen and went out a side door in the hallway. It led to the back of the firehouse.

Immediately as they cleared the door, Cade asked, "What do you want, Madson?"

"I've heard that you took Mary out on Saturday."

Cade kept silent. *Everyone* knew he and Mary had gone out. He didn't have time for the obvious. His look conveyed his thoughts.

Matt continued, "I know you like her," Matt rolled his eyes and said with feeling, "*Everyone* likes her. But I think she and I make a better couple than *you and Mary*."

"You've already told me this bullshit. What do you want?"

"As you know, women in our age group in this area are few and far between. The good ones are married or taken. Mary should date me. We're more compatible than you and Mary."

Cade's brow furrow. "How did you come by this pearl of wisdom? Because as far as I know, Mary doesn't know anything about herself before coming to Eldred. And since she's been here, she's shown an interest in books, kids, and her community. I'm the sheriff, and I love kids and this community."

Matt scowled. "You know what I am talking about."

Cade took a threatening step closer, getting in Matt's face. "Yeah, I do know what you mean. You mean the same thing as those racists assholes who say people shouldn't date outside their race, dirtying up the gene pool by creating mixed babies, some nonsense like that."

Genuine surprise flashed across Matt's face. "That's different. I am not racists!"

"Really? Because, from where I am standing, y'all look identical. I don't need or seek your permission to date someone I am interested in. And, the one person's permission I do need, gave it. It was the same person who told you no. She made her feelings known on the subject, and now I have. Goodbye, Matt." Cade did an about-face with those final words and went through the firehouse to exit the way he entered.

Outside, unaware, Cade slammed his SUV's door. Marshal Duncan looked over at him from the passenger seat. "Everything alright?"

Putting his shades on and backing out of the parking spot, Cade pictured Mary's sweet smiles from their date, rather than Matt's scowling one of moments ago, answering the Marshal, "Everything is fine."

∞∞∞∞

Mary Smith pulled the keys to the library's front door out of her hefty purse. Breathing in the brisk cool air, she smiled. Another *new* like. She loved cool crisp fall air. It was pleasing to her senses.

Mary walked from the library's employee parking lot in the back of the library. She liked the quiet of early mornings too. Her smile grew as she realized the immense joy she felt from re-learning about the things she liked.

Thirteen months ago, she woke up in a strange hospital bed, hurt and traumatized without a single memory. She had thought her life was over and that she would never like anything again. But then her eyes had connected with the most compelling, bluest, compassionate, honest-looking eyes she had ever seen. Well, that she had seen thus far.

Sheriff Cade Myers had been her quiet in the storm, her still waters in a riotous sea. He made her feel safe when she was scared. And she had no clue as to why she should be afraid. He had calming confidence about him that put her unease at rest. It didn't hurt that he was also one of the finest looking men she had ever come across in her short memory. Although Mary didn't need her memories to know that Cade was exceptional in the looks category. She merely had to see the way every woman, young or old, married or single, responded to him.

If she didn't have all that to help clue her into how incredibly good-looking Cade is, she only had to register her own body's reactions. His muscular physique, strongly chiseled jaw, firm lips, and sexy penetrating, seemingly all-knowing, blue eyes caused Mary's nether regions to clench when he spoke in his deep baritone. And her heart stuttered when he walked in a room. She deeply inhaled when around him because his scent was divine.

Unlocking the front double doors and then the inner doors, Mary flicked the row of light switches to the right of the entrance. Nothing happened. Frowning, she tried the switches again. Other than the clicking sounds, there was nothing.

She walked further into the library's main entrance, listening for any sound. Hearing nothing, she walked to the large circulation counter, placing her purse, lunch bag, and keys down on the empty surface. She walked past several tables and chairs, a small sofa, and the elevator to the first row of books, walking to the end towards the fuse box.

As she reached the end of the row, her steps slowed. Her flesh began to crawl, and the hairs on the back of her neck stood on end.

The creepily whispered, "Marrry." Froze her in place.

SLAM!

Startled, Mary jumped. The repeated whisper caused her feet to start moving again, turn around, heading back towards the circulation counter. She came up fast on the desk, skidding to a halt as her eyes took in the only item on its surface. A pink flower. Her personal items were gone.

"Marrry." The whisper sounded again. She did a slow circle. She couldn't tell where it was coming from.

SLAM!

All Mary knew was that she was no longer alone. She had to get out of the library. The front entrance loomed invitingly in front of her. One of her many lost memories was any movies she had seen. But there was a genre of movies she had grown a liking for in her thirteen months of memory. Horror-slasher films. She watched them all with a macabre fascination. They all had one thing in common. The dumb victim being led to the front door to be ambushed by the killer. Mary shook her head and turned, running towards the farthest row of books. At the end of the last row was the back door.

Mary picked up speed to full-out running as the sounds grew louder and closer.

SLAM!

SLAM!

SLAM!

Mary skidded and scrambled, falling to the floor in her attempt to stop her full speed ahead to the back door. From the floor, she looked up at the fully black-clad figure blocking the back door. His imposing stance had her turning while still on the floor and attempting to get her feet under her so she could get her ass off the ground. Her foot was grabbed in a tight grip. Mary looked over her shoulder into a face of complete blackness. She screamed at the top of her lungs, kicking her feet.

She landed a well-placed kick to the figure's head. He let go of her foot. Without hesitation, Mary got on her feet and took off in the direction she had come. Looking over her shoulder, she spotted the man in pursuit. She screamed and switched her direction again, going down one of the other rows, keeping her gaze over her shoulder, making sure she was maintaining distance between her and her dark pursuer.

With her attention intently behind her, shockwaves went through her entire body when she crashed into a solid wall. Mary's screams became genuinely horrified. Restraining arms locked around her, she beat uselessly at the ungiving wall.

"Mary! Mary!"

Mary was in such a state she didn't hear the words coming from somewhere outside her panic.

"Mary! Mary! It's Cade! Mary, sweetheart, it's Cade!"

Cade shook a completely terrified Mary, trying to get her whole awareness. "Mary, it's Cade Myers!"

Suddenly, she stopped beating against his chest and looking over her shoulder. She went still and looked up into Cade's face. Locking onto his beautiful blue eyes, in a small voice laced with fear, she questioned, "Cade?"

He gave her a gentle smile. "Yes, it's me, sweetheart."

With a deep shudder, she collapsed against his chest, wrapping her arms around him, holding on tight. "Oh, C-cade." She hiccupped and sighed.

Cade held her tightly to him, asking, "What is it? What's wrong!"

Leaning away from him, tears streaming down her face, she pointed over her shoulder. "*He* was right behind me."

Instantly, Cade switched to his police persona. He gently pushed her towards the front. "Go out the front doors to my car."

Making sure Mary started towards the front, Cade started towards the back door as he heard it bang shut. Unsnapping the strap on his holstered gun, he cautiously approached the door. Opening it in slow increments, peeking out and spotting a fast-moving figure in all black, Cade gave chase, running hard and fast to catch up.

From several paces behind, Cade took note, the black-clad man was smaller than him, almost slight of build and the fucker was fast. Cade poured on the speed as they traversed the back parking lot towards the woods. Cade deduced that the asshole was heading in the woods to get to the road that came out the other side.

Proving Cade's guess correct, the figure sped up and entered the woods at neck-break speed, causing Cade to lose sight of him.

Cade pulled his weapon and ran harder, entering the woods. He looked around, stopping for several seconds to listen. Hearing his suspect's mad dash through the foliage, slapping leaves and snapping twigs, Cade ran after him.

Cade put on enough speed to get eyes on the perp again as he crashed through the last of the woods up ahead. As Cade was coming to the end of the woods, he heard a car door slam. Cade burst through the last of the trees as an engine roared to life. He spied a black Ford four by four speeding away. Cade took aim, firing at the tires unsuccessfully as it got smaller in the distance.

Swearing, Cade keyed the mic on his shoulder, panting, he talked into it, "Zebra1 to Zebra33."

"Zebra3-3 here."

"I'm 10-57, 10-66 at the library."

"Copy, 10-49."

"Dispatch?"

"Right here, Sheriff. Whatcha need?" Sally's smooth tone called through his radio.

"Put a BOLO out on a black Ford Four by Four with a chrome gun rack, partial plate ADAM-DAVID-FRANK-ONE."

"Copy that, Sheriff."

Cade holstered his weapon as he continued to stare in the direction of the disappearing black Ford truck. Shaking his head, he took a deep breath and turned to make his way back to the library. It looked like Mary's stalker had just amped up his obsession with her.

Chapter 3

Mary nervously sat in the front of Cade's police vehicle. Her stomach was in knots until she heard his deep baritone over the radio. However, her shakes didn't cease until she saw his tall, muscular frame walk out of the library's front doors. She quickly opened the car door, leaving it standing open, she ran to Cade.

Cade caught her in his arms, pulling her in tight as she laid her head against his chest and wrapped her arms around him.

"Oh, God, Cade! I was so scared."

He gently stroked her back. "He got away, but I promise you, I'll get him."

She looked up, and his gaze locked on hers. They stared into one another's eyes. Mary felt their connection sizzling between. By mutual silent consent, they reached for each other. Cade lowered his head, and Mary stood on her toes. Their lips made soft contact, and their connection intensified.

Mary moaned and gasped, allowing Cade's tongue to enter her mouth. He felt the electricity that was between them. The same electricity he felt when she first opened her eyes and looked deeply, trustingly into his. As he emitted his own moan, Cade was blown away by his feelings for the woman in arms.

Their tongues twirled sexily, causing Cade to growl and end their kiss by giving her bottom lip a final gentle swipe with his tongue. With his forehead against hers and his eyes shut tight, trying to get his body under control, he whispered, "Baby, you do me in. I have to be the sheriff right now when all I want to be is your man and take you away from here."

Mary leaned back to look at him, touching her lip where he had last stroked his tongue. Her look was one of wonder. Cade had witnessed enough of Mary's re-do firsts looks. They had ranged from a slight frown, a mild smile to a downright grossed-out frown and furrow, to an awestruck look of wonder and pleasantly surprised. She was wearing her pleasantly surprised look. Her pleased looks had a way of puffing his chest in male pride. Their first kiss on their first date had raised her eyebrows in shock. She gasped the back of his head and demanded in a sweet tone, "Do that again."

The woman had a way of making a man feel as though he was magical or something. Cade was no exception. His smile turned a bit cocky as she continued to stare at him in wonder, her eyes lingering on his mouth.

"Another new feeling?" Cade asked. His words filled with teasing gentleness.

Slowly nodding, her fingers left her lips and reached up and stroked his. "Your mouth is incredible. It makes me feel *so* good. I went from totally terrified to my nipples growing hard and wanting to do more kissing."

Cade choked back laughter as her hand left his mouth to rest on his chest. He pulled her back into his arms. "I am glad I am giving you these new feelings, and you find them so enjoyable." His voice grew gravelly, "I am thrilled you said yes to me and no to all those other guys. I couldn't be happier I am your do-over *firsts*."

She leaned back to catch his gaze with hers. She had a look of dawning realization. "Are you telling me any guy I go out with and kiss will bring about the same feeling?"

Cade lost his desire to laugh or tease her. Narrowing his eyes, he told her the truth. "Hell no! Trust me, baby, what we feel when we kiss is rare. It doesn't feel the same with everyone."

She nodded and laid her head back on his chest, squeezing him to her. "I am glad too."

"I'm glad I got here in enough time to stop whatever that asshole had in mind."

On autopilot, Mary touched a finger to his lips. "Don't cuss."

Cade watched Mary's eyes widen in shock. He could tell she was surprised. He figured it was her past persona acting on instinct when she did things out of the blue like that. Apparently, her past self didn't swear.

He smiled gently. "I'll try not to around you."

Shaking off her confusion over her unintentional action, she asked, "Why are you here so fortuitously?" Glancing at the watch on her slender wrist, she added, "You're normally at the station at this time."

"I wanted to check on you. Sally told me you got something from your stalker on your door last night."

Nodding, Mary confirmed. "He left a pink flower on my backdoor. It's identical to the one on the counter in the library."

Just then, deputies Harold Boyd and Larry Struthers pulled into the parking lot, each parking their police cars on either side of Cade's SUV. They both hopped out, walking directly to Cade. The three went immediately into police mode.

Later, Mary sat at the circulation counter watching the forensic techs bag items out of place around the library. Apparently, the sounds Mary had heard when her stalker was harassing her was the sound of books being slammed onto the floor. Cade had called in the state police forensic team, hoping they could get prints from one of the items. He told her that the odds were slim but worth the cost if there were prints.

She had been outside for a while after the deputies first arrived. She had felt reluctant to release her hold on Cade. But she knew he had to do his sheriff duties regardless of her feelings of need. Cade and the deputies went off to inspect the library and its perimeter. At the same time, she had spent over twenty minutes turning patrons away, explaining that the library was closed until further notice.

Lana Miles had left the school to check in on her. She came running up to Mary.

"Mary, what is going on? You okay? Miss Purn came to the school to pick up her grandson because he threw up getting off the bus this morning and said there was a bunch of cop cars here."

Since deciding to stay in Eldred after establishing her new identity, Mary had become close with two of the elementary school's employees. Lana Miles, a secretary in the main office, and Mandy Odessa, a teacher.

She gave Lana a shaky smile. "It's okay. Nothing too serious. I just got scared."

Lana looked around at the cop cars and the state police's van. "Seems like a lot of trouble for 'nothing too serious."

"Someone was in the library when I arrived. He scared me. Cad-, uh, I mean, Sheriff Myers interrupted the guy, whatever he was doing. The sheriff gave chase out the backdoor, but the guy got away."

Lana's eyes got big. "Wow! I tell ya, this town was pretty sleepy until you and Sheriff Myers showed up." At Mary's worried frown, Lana clarified, "Oh, honey, I didn't mean that the way it sounded. Don't worry. I am sure Sherif- I mean, Cade will get the creep pretty soon."

Mary smiled at Lana's teasing about her hesitation over calling Cade by his first name.

"I just don't want to be disrespectful. He's here in his sheriff capacity, not—"

"Not the sexy, drool-worthy, hot bod, boyfriend capacity?" Lana laughed as Mary blushed.

Soon after, Lana left, promising to be by Mary's place later with takeout and ready to hear about her date with Cade this past Saturday.

Now, from her vantage point behind the counter, she watched the activity and sneaked peeks at Cade. He was easily the best-looking and most impressive man in the room, both physically and in demeanor. He was in charge, but he wasn't overbearing about it. He had kindness in his directions. He made his orders sound like he was seeking a favor. Mary got the sense that it could change quickly if needed.

On their date, he had been the consummate gentleman, impeccable manners. Even at the end when he had taken her in his arms to kiss her. He had ensured Mary's permission before proceeding to blow her top and curl her toes with his kiss. She couldn't wait to get even closer with Cade.

"Mary. Thank Goodness." The words brought Mary's concentrated attention and thoughts from Cade's sexiness to Matt Madson's worried gaze.

Mary didn't know what to make of him. She got a strange vibe from Matt. He seemed to be always on the verge of saying something, and then whatever comes out of his mouth is something other than what his look implied. It was the strangest feeling Mary had gotten from anyone else in town. There was something that didn't quite ring true about him. It was the reason she didn't accept his offer of a date. Well, that, and the fact that she hadn't been drawn to anyone other than Cade.

Looking at Matt now, she got the same odd feeling of something being not quite right. Something she couldn't put her finger on but nagged at the back of her consciousness. For example, the intense concern on his face, why was it even there to that degree. Mary was far closer with Lana and, of course, Cade, and neither's concern appeared *this* strong.

Mary got the suspicion that Matt would have pulled her into his arms if the circulation counter weren't separating them. Frowning, she stood and took a small step back, putting even more space between them.

"Matt, hello. What are you doing here?"

"What do you mean? I heard over the Lt.'s radio all the different departments being dispatched here." Matt gave her a for-shame look. "Of course, I'd come to make sure you're okay."

Mary didn't know what to say. She continued to frown at him in silence, puzzling over his actions. He acted as though they were in a relationship. Hmm, strange.

Mary gave him a reluctant smile and said, "I-I am alright. Thank you, Matt."

Matt looked around at the activity and suggested, "Why don't you let me take you home? Obviously, the library is closed for the day."

Mary was shocked. Not knowing what to say, she nervously wiped her hands down her sides and stuttered, "Oh-t-that's al—"

"Mary is fine, Madson. I'll take her home when I am done here." Cade's tone was cool as he walked up to the counter.

Matt's look turned irritated as he insisted. "I can take her."

"It's not necessary." Cade was just as insistent.

Mary's eyes ping-ponged between them. They seemed to be playing a game among themselves. A game that had absolutely nothing to do with her.

"Uh, that's okay, gentlemen. I drove here. I can get myself home when I am ready."

The two men glared at one another for several seconds more before turning much gentler gazes toward her.

Cade smiled and gave her a wink. "Okay."

Matt's mouth slanted in a smile a little less appealing than Cade's and offered, "I can wait and follow you to make sure you get there safely."

Frowning deeply, Mary was at a loss in what else to say to Matt.

Cade wasn't. "She already has a stalker, thanks, but no thanks."

Matt turned an angry face to Cade. "I was making the offer as a friend. What's the matter?" Matt smirked. "Hotshot Sheriff can't handle the competition?"

With an unworried chuckled, Cade answered. "From where I am standing, there is none." Giving Mary one last wink, he turned his back on Matt, returning to the group of state lab guys.

Matt's eyes narrowed in dislike at Cade's back. He turned around to find Mary looking at him in disapproval. He quickly fixed his features. "I really don't mind waiting. I'll sit outside until you're ready."

Matt turned, walking out the door, not waiting for Mary to answer one way or another. Shaking her head, she sat and waited until Cade said it was okay to leave.

Cade watched Madson leave. He smirked, half-listening to the state lab techs tell him his chances of getting anything concrete from their evidence gathering was slim to nil. Cade already knew it was a long shot. But he figured it couldn't hurt.

Madson was annoying as hell. Mary made it plain who she wanted to date. What was his problem? Cade couldn't figure out why he changed so drastically from the buddy he used to hang out with to the racist asshole he was now. Of course, his attitude change had to do with him wanting Mary too. But he didn't understand Madson's belief that he should be with Mary instead based on race. It was a ridiculous, antiquated ideology. Cade had no plans to stop dating Mary. Madson could go pound sand.

Cade sighed. He had too much going on to worry about Madson's racist ass. He had to stop the Red X Prankster, find Mandy Odessa, arrest Mary's stalker, stop a possible hitman and still find time to handle the uptick in minor crime for the holidays. Halloween was in three days. He had to wrap some of this shit up. He was looking forward to spending the holidays getting to know Mary and getting closer to her.

He glanced over and found her watching him with an expression on her face he was beginning to like a lot. It was filled with admiration, feminine approval with a hint of lust. Oh, hell, yeah. Cade wanted to explore this new thing between him and Mary.

Seeing motion in his peripheral, his attention left Mary's beautiful face to the front door of the library. Marshal Duncan entered, stopping a few feet in until he spotted Cade and walked over.

"Sheriff, I rechecked Mandy Odessa's place. She's not there. The car is gone. There is not much else I can do until someone has a sighting or knows her location."

"You're heading out?" Cade asked.

"I'm going to stay for a few days and search, see if I can get a handle on her timeline, specifically the twenty-four hours before the last time she was seen."

"My deputies and I will keep an eye out for her."

Offering his hand, Marshal Duncan added, "I appreciate it. I am staying at the Motor Inn out on the highway right before you enter the town."

Cade shook his hand. "I know it." Tapping a finger to his hat in way of goodbye, he watched Marshal Duncan leave.

Cade walked over to Mary, loving that her smile grew with each step he made.

"So, do you want to hang out for a bit here until I am done overseeing the scene, or do you want one of my men to take you home? He'll be stationed outside your house until I get there."

Mary's smile held an inviting warmth, her delicious lips parted slightly as if she were gasping in surprise. Cade nearly groaned, thinking about tasting her mouth and making her gasp again. Mary's eyelashes fluttered down shyly like she knew what he was thinking.

Softly she said, "I'll wait for you."

With his signature wink and a smile, he turned back to his job.

∞∞∞∞

Casey Tillman and Kallie Kramer walked up the steep hill.

Puffing and stopping every few steps, Kallie asked in an annoyed tone, "How much further?"

"You'd get up the hill with less strain if you'd shut up and just walk."

Flipping Casey the bird, Kallie stomped her next few feet. He got on her last nerve. He had said it was a short walk. What they were actually doing was climbing. And there was nothing short about it in Kallie's book. What was she doing out here anyway? Her inner voice answered her. *You wanted a date for the Halloween Dance and decided Casey Tillman was a good choice.*

Huffing and puffing audibly, Kallie panted out, "Why do we have to go so high up?"

Without turning around, Casey said in a long measured tone, "The people in charge of town planning stuff put it up here so it wouldn't have easy access."

"If..." puff, huff, "...it's so..." huff, puff, "...hard to get..." puff, huff, "...to, how are you gonna access it?"

This time Casey did turn around, holding a ring with a bunch of keys aloft. "I have my brother's keys from the firehouse. His Lt. fills in at the power company as an electrical engineer, so he has all access to stuff like this. A few months ago, there was a fire at the gas station, and there was a down powerline, and the Lt. sent my brother to come to turn off the power from this manual switch. I was with him. Later at home, I swiped the keys. My brother thought he lost them."

Standing still, Kallie eyed Casey with a bit of worry. "You've been planning this for months?"

Casey rolled his eyes. "No, stupid. I just thought of it. I just took the keys because," He shrugged. "I don't know. Just in case."

Kallie nodded her understanding, not understanding at all. "Okay, so why are we doing this again?"

"It'll be fun to see them run around looking for the cause before they think of the transfer switch up here."

Shaking her head, Kallie told him a home truth. "Your idea of fun isn't fun."

"Just stop talking so you can walk better. For a girl with a nice bod, you sure suck at physical stuff."

All Kallie heard was nice bod. "You think I have a nice body?"

Casey rolled his eyes again, pulling his hoodie over his head and the front up over his nose. "Come on, cover yourself. We're almost there."

With a long-suffering sigh, Kallie did as she was told. Casey told her to dress in all black and wear a hoodie, not her all too identifiable pink coat. She stomped behind Casey, grumbling about the incline when he finally stopped in front of a fence that looked like it was built into the hillside. It enclosed a small concrete structure with lead pipes coming from the ground into a huge black metal box.

Casey used the keys on the large padlock on the fence's entrance. He turned and smiled, holding the lock triumphantly in the air.

Kallie shook her head. "Now what?"

Casey grinned evilly as he took out a spray can of red paint.

"Now the fun begins."

Chapter 4

"So, Matt just sat in the car waiting for you all that time?" Lana asked Mary while pulling a piece of pizza out of the fully-loaded pie she brought over to Mary's.

"Oh, my, God, yes," Mary said, also serving herself pizza. "It was the strangest thing. I don't even know why he showed up in the first place."

Lana laughed, swallowed her pizza, and took a sip of soda. "Because he's hot for you, Mary. He's probably having those buttoned-up librarians transformed to sex-kitten fantasies about you."

"Oh, no, I hope not." Mary shook her head.

"Might as well get used to it." Lana's mouth slanted in a resigned smile. "It's most likely a case of you getting re-used to it. Because your looks haven't changed. You were a hottie before you lost your memory."

Mary shook her head and drank some of her water before replying. "Well, it feels new to me. It's crazy to me that all the available men asked me out back to back. I'm mean, one right after the other. I was feeling a little overwhelmed. And Matt Madson is just a little too intense for me."

"Around here, a woman not taken already or ready for the nursing home is a rare thing. And one as beautiful as you? Forget about it. You're like fresh blood to rabid dogs."

Mary frowned. "Gee, thanks. You make me sound like a piece of meat."

Lana laughed and winked. "Hey, I'm talking only Grade-A pure beef, baby."

Mary laughed, waving a hand at her friend's silliness. Then she sobered. "But there is something about Matt I can't put my finger on. Cade would be even longer, so I decided one of his men should bring me home instead of me waiting for him, longer than I already had. Cade walked me to my car and then told Matt that he needn't follow since Deputy Struthers was seeing me home."

Between bites, Lana asked, "Aww, how did poor Matt take it not driving you home?"

Mary's eyes widened incredulously. "That's just it; he followed me anyway. Well, he followed us. He was behind the deputy's car."

Lana was shocked. "Now, that's strange." She shook her head. "I don't remember him being coo-coo for cocoa puffs before."

"That's not comforting."

Lana grinned and joked. "He wants to have sex with you something bad."

"I am not having sex with Matt Madson!"

"Glad to hear it."

Both women were startled. Mary gasped, and Lana yelped, spilling her entire cup of soda.

"God, damn it, Cade!" Lana exclaimed, throwing napkins on the fast-growing puddle of soda. She threw a glare at

Cade standing in Mary's living room archway. "You scared the crap out of me."

Recovered from her shock, Mary went to Cade with a smile. "Hello."

He took her in his arms, looking at her face. Liking the welcoming warmth she exuded, he smiled. "Hello to you."

They leaned into a kiss simultaneously. Mary moaned against his mouth. Cade felt the same way. He pulled back slowly, then put his mouth against her ear and whispered so only Mary could hear. "I want the pleasure of re-introducing you to love making."

Mary put her arms around his neck, bringing his mouth back down to hers. She kissed him slowly, deeply. This time Cade groaned before giving her bottom lip one last swipe with his tongue.

Touching his forehead to hers, he whispered. "Baby, you do me in."

"Guys, get a room." Lana joked.

"We plan to." Cade joked back.

Mary moved her hand to Cade's chest. "Want some pizza and wings? There are some garlic knots too."

Cade nodded. "I could eat."

Mary took his hand and led him to the sofa next to her spot. She fixed him a plate, pointing a finger to items laid out on the table, and added them to his plate as he nodded.

"So, it's true. You women talk about men and sex all the time when we men are not around."

Mary put napkins and a can of cola in Cade's reach and retook her seat.

"No, we don't. You just happened to come in when sex was mentioned." Lana corrected Cade, re-filling her cup with soda.

Mary looked at Cade. "I was just explaining how Matt's intenseness around me creeps me out a little."

Cade frowned, swallowing before saying. "Yea, I don't remember him ever being like that."

Lana added her two cents. "Not only did he spend all that time hanging outside waiting for Mary, do you know, he still followed her home even though you had Deputy Struthers follow her?"

Cade set his plate down, scowling. "Annoying fucker."

Immediately, Mary placed a gentle finger across Cade's lips. "Don't cuss."

Cade watched Mary slowly lower her hand, looking at it as if it belonged to someone else or had moved entirely without her knowledge.

He had seen that confused look cross her beautiful features many times since she woke up in the hospital bed. She was puzzling over her automatic reaction to something. Cade figured that it was a habit so ingrained that she did it without thought, without memory. If he were a betting man, he'd bet pre-memory-loss Mary didn't use foul language and had been around someone who swore a lot, and she was in the habit of telling them to stop by placing her finger across their lips. He was more concerned about who she had done it to. Placing your finger across someone's lips was an intimate action. An action a lover or a parent did. Cade wondered in which role Mary used the gesture in the past.

Forgetting his worry over whether the woman he was falling for was a *mother* or *wife*, he smiled gently at her, taking the hand she was still staring at. "Okay, I'll try around you."

"I was telling her that Matt is hot for her sexy bod." Lana had also noticed Mary's look of surprise over her action. She worried about her friend. It was always in the back of Lana's mind that they had become best friends because someone had beaten Mary and left her for dead on the side of the road like garbage.

Losing her worrisome look, Mary shook her head. "No, it's more than that. He acts like we know each other. He takes our interactions much more personally than it is. Like at the library today. There was no reason for him to be there. We don't know each other like that."

A crease appeared on Lana's forehead before she glanced at Mary, switching her gaze to Cade. "Could he know Mary from before?"

Cade shook his head in the negative. "No, way. He'd have used his familiarity with her to situate himself in a better position in her life. Right now, whether he realizes it or not, he's only on the outskirt of Mary's life."

"Could he be Mary's stalker?" Lana suggested.

Mary's eyes grew wide as her gaze sought Cade's.

Reluctantly, he negated that idea. "No. He wouldn't do that even though he's acting out of character." Cade smirked and added. "Besides, I think he was with me when Mary received one of her heavy-breather calls from her stalker."

Cade saw Mary's shoulders slump in defeat. He decided to relieve some of her worries. "I think I know why he's so...not Matt."

Both women stared at him in anticipation. "What?" They asked simultaneously.

With a resigned sigh, Cade explained. "It's because you're black."

Lana's eyes bugged out. "Uh, so is *he*!"

Mary interpreted Cade's look. Glancing at her friend, she said, "That's it, Lana." She looked back at Cade. "That's really it, isn't it? Because I am black."

"What?" Lana was confused.

Sparing Lana a quick glance before looking back at Mary and gently squeezing her hand, Cade explained. "He thinks you and he should be dating because you both are black, no mixing of the races."

"What in the jumped-up-Jesus, backward-thinking, outdated, Jim Crow, cult-like, bullshit is this?"

Mary frowned sadly. "I knew I was getting a strange vibe off him. I didn't think it was this. It's crazy."

Cade nodded. "Before this issue of dating you came up, I never would have guessed either. We've always got alon—"

Suddenly, the lights went out, engulfing them in complete darkness, Lana yelped, and Mary gasped. With the darkness came silence.

Cade took the mag-light from his belt, pointing it towards the floor.

"Okay, lend me your flashlight, and I'll go to the basement and check the fuse box," Mary said.

Cade's voice came out of the darkness. He was moving towards the window. "No, it's not just you. Look outside." He pointed his light on the path to the window. When Mary stood beside him, he added. "Besides, even if it were just you, I wouldn't lend you my flashlight to go to the basement by yourself. I'd go there myself."

Cade keyed the mic on his shoulder. "Sally, get Deputy Struthers back out to Mary's and call in Deputy Lockhart and put the state police on alert. We might need to have them assist as Eldred is experiencing some kind of outage."

"Copy that. It's all over, Sheriff?" Sally's voice came over Cade's radio.

Talking into his mic, he answered Sally. "I'm guessing, but I think so. I'm headed back to the main street. This is an invitation to restless teens and ne'er do wells, especially the Red X prankster."

"Copy that, Sheriff."

Cade turned from the window, addressing Mary. "I'll need to leave as soon as Struthers gets here."

"Don't be silly. You should go now. I'll be alright the fifteen or twenty minutes it will take Struthers to get here. The town needs you." Mary insisted.

"Hey, what am I? Chopped liver? I can stay with her until the deputy gets here."

Cade placed his flashlight in Mary's hand, took her other one in his, and led her back to the sofa. "Are you guys sure?"

"Of course," Mary said.

"Go on, get outta here." Lana agreed.

Instinctively he found Mary's mouth in the darkness. He quickly brushed her lips with his. "Thank you for dinner. Is it alright if I come back when we get the power restored?"

"Of course." She smiled even though he couldn't see it.

Cade felt her smile and brushed his thumb across her bottom lip with a low groan. "I don't know what time it will be, but I *will* be back."

"Yeah, we get it. You're coming back to get in some make-out time." Lana laughed.

Mary sent a censorious look at Lana that she had no way of seeing.

Cade laughed, kissing Mary one last time before taking his leave.

∞∞∞∞

"What the hell is going on here, Sheriff?" Mayor Oliver 'Olly' Bonner yelled over the persistent ringing of the phones on several desks and the overall busy sounds of the overwhelmed sheriff's station. All the clerks, the other dispatcher, and all the deputies were on deck. Right now, they were handling an unusual amount of calls. Everyone was worried about the outage. The sheriff's station was on a backup generator.

"Olly, we're working on it. I called in Tim Mendelson. He's working with the power company to restore the power. First, they gotta find out what happened."

The portly mayor pulled a handkerchief from his suit pocket, wiping a brow saturated in sweat. Cade shook his head. The mayor tended to sweat when he was worried. It certainly wasn't hot enough to sweat so profusely.

"Mayor, is there something specific I can do for you? As you can see, we're being swamped. My deputies are spread all over the county putting out fires."

"My God! There are fires as in plural?" Olly looked as if he were about to have a stroke.

"Easy, Mayor. I meant the metaphorical fires, not actual fires."

Placing a dramatic hand against his heart, he sighed in relief. "Thank goodness. I came by to see if you need anything."

"I got this, Mayor. Don't worry."

Taking a long look at Cade, the mayor nodded in approval. "You know I wasn't sure about you when we hired you. You seemed too young for the job. I am happily surprised by your ability to handle whatever comes your way. I know there is a rise in petty crimes near Halloween. You handled your first year amazingly well." He looked around at the busy yet orderly station. "I guess I'll leave you to it, get out of your hair. Remember to call if you need anything."

Sally called to Cade as the Mayor left. "Cade, you need to get someone over to the high school. There is an unknown disturbance."

"I'll go. Everyone else is out doing something."

"You want me to pull Struthers from Mary's place, send him?"

"No. Leave him there. This is the perfect opportunity for her stalker to try something. It's no problem. I'll go."

∞∞∞∞

Besides the lack of light, Cade knew there was something else wrong at the school. The main doors stood wide open, and the fire alarm was going off. Just as he stepped out of his car, he heard a fire truck's siren in the distance.

There were no apparent signs of a fire, no smell of smoke, nor any visual indications of smoke. Cade pulled out his borrowed flashlight. He left his with Mary. He walked to the door, entering slowly. He heard music coming from one of the offices. He unsnapped his holster, resting his hand on his gun.

Several feet before the office door, Cade's feet slipped. Catching himself before he went down, he shined his flashlight at the floor. A large puddle of dark red blood was pooled in front of the office door. Cade pulled his gun free of its holster and crossed his wrists, aiming the weapon with the flashlight on top. He proceeded carefully into the office.

There was Halloween music playing on a loop. The fire alarm was deafening at this point. Cade flashed his light around, taking in the office, revealing corners. He startled when his light beam picked up a figure sitting at the office desk.

"Hands in the air!"

The figure didn't move. Heart thudding faster, Cade advanced further into the room. "Let me see your fucking hands! Now!"

As he got closer, Cade realized the figure was covered in blood. Moving cautiously closer, he reached out for what was left of the figure's neck for his pulse. It was merely a formality. Cade knew the person was dead. Half his face was missing.

Chapter 5

Hearing running footsteps headed towards the office, Cade aimed his gun and flashlight at the office doorway. The steps slipped and slide for a second in the blood and then stopped. Someone loomed in the entrance.

"Police! Freeze!"

"Fuck! Jesus Christ, don't shoot! Sheriff Myers, it's me! Billy Tillman!"

Cade directed his light to Billy's face. The young man was holding his hands up in a staying motion.

Cade shouted over the alarm. "Shit. What are you doing here?"

Billy yelled back. "We're respond—" The abrupt cessation of the fire alarm gave both occupants in the room pause.

Cade holstered his weapon and pointed the flashlight to the floor. "What made you come to the office?"

"I saw the arc of your light." Billy lowered his hands.

"Paramedics and firefighters are supposed to wait for the police to secure a suspicious scene before entering."

"Sorry, we saw your car out front. I thought it could be where the fire origin was located."

"Who else is with you?"

"Matt is subbing for Tim, who is with the power company trying to get power restored. It's Matt and me until we checked it out. The rest of the team is on standby."

"Where's Matt?"

"He went to shut off the alarm."

"Well, there isn't any fire here. This is officially a crime scene. I need you and Matt to step outside."

"We're not leaving until I determine there is no fire," Matt said, joining Billy in the doorway.

Cade narrowed his eyes at Matt. "There is no fire. I am the sheriff of this county, and you'll do as I say."

Matt scoffed. "During a fire emergency, as acting supervisor, I outrank you and the mayor himself."

Cade wasn't about to have a pissing contest with Madson. He moved toward the firemen, stopping short of getting in their personal space. "I think the words you need to concentrate on in that sentence are 'During a fire emergency.' There is no fire emergency. However, there is a police one. Step outside, gentlemen, now!"

Billy didn't hesitate, turning to leave immediately. Matt stared at Cade in a challenging manner. Cade didn't feel the need to repeat himself. He let his silence and stance convey that Matt left now on his own power or got forcibly taken out. Cade made sure, even in the dark, his expression told Matt that he wouldn't like the latter choice.

∞∞∞∞

"Lana, you really didn't have to stay if you need to get home."

"Get home to what?" Lana waved her hand at Mary. Belatedly, remembering Mary probably couldn't see the gesture. "I didn't have anything planned. Girl, I'm fine."

Mary sat on her sofa with the flashlight on the table, pointing towards a wall. "Good. I was lying. I'd really like you to stay."

"You don't have to put on a brave face for me. We're besties."

Mary sighed in relief. "Thank you for saying that. I feel like I've been taken care of ever since I woke up in the hospital. I want everyone to know I am a capable person. I don't need to be coddled."

"Mary, everyone, and I do mean everyone, in this town absolutely loves you and thinks you're a strong person. Jesus, most people would have balled up into the fetal position and never come out if they went through what you did. I don't know how you were before, but now I see a person I like and admire. An incredible survivor."

Mary smiled, feeling her cheeks heat. She changed the subject, standing, "I was hoping the lights would be on soon. But we've sat in the dark long enough. Help me find some candles and light them, get some light in this place."

"Great. Let's do it." Lana was enthusiastic.

Mary handed the flashlight to Lana, grabbing her cellphone off the coffee table. "Here, use this. I'll use my cell's flashlight. You check under the sink in the downstairs bathroom. I keep scented candles there. Light one in there too. I'll go check in the kitchen and light some in there as well."

Lana put the flashlight back on the table. "Let's leave the flashlight here on the table to help light up this room. I'll use my cell too."

The women went off in separate directions. As Mary reached the kitchen, her cellphone rang and vibrated in her hand. Looking at the caller ID, she couldn't stop the smile from spreading across her face.

"Hello." She said, breathless with excitement.

"Hello to you." Cade's sexy baritone sent a pleasant tingle down her spine.

"Are you all right? Figured out what happened with the lights?" Mary held the phone between her chin and shoulder, leaving her hands free to rummage through her 'everything' drawer under the long kitchen counter.

"Tim is on the power outage problem. I've encountered another problem."

"Oh, something I can help you with?" Mary asked as she closed one drawer and opened another.

"No, sweetheart. I am just calling to let you know I probably will not make it back to your place tonight."

Brow furrowing, she closed the last drawer under the counter and headed to check her pantry. "Are you okay?"

"Yes, I am. It's a police matter I need to handle myself. I am calling to get a raincheck for tomorrow night."

"A raincheck? For dinner?"

Cade's voice dropped an octave. "For dinner, after dinner, all of what tonight entailed. I was looking forward to holding you in my arms for more than a brief moment and getting some more of those incredible kisses you give."

"Me? Your kisses curl my toes. It's amazing how you make me feel."

Mary opened the pantry. It was narrow with shelves on either side. She walked down the aisle, remembering there was a box with candles in it on the bottom shelf all the way inside.

Cade's voice kept her company as she walked to the end, knelt, and moved can goods out of the way to reach the box.

"Uh, huh. Can you guess which part of my body your kisses affect besides my toes?" Cade's timber got even lower.

Mary grabbed the box of tapered candles and stood to leave the pantry. Her voice took on a sultry lilt. "Why Sheriff Myers I d—"

Suddenly, Mary screamed, dropping her phone and the box of candles. A shadowy form stood on the pantry threshold. Remembering she wasn't alone in the house, she knelt, giving a nervous laugh. "Lana, you scared me."

Her phone-back had come off, and the battery separated, the candles were scattered about. She kept meaning to get a case for her phone but never did. Draped in the darkness, she felt around for her phone while gathering up candles. "You didn't find any candles in the bathroom?"

Mary had several candles and her phone in her hand, feeling around for the battery when she realized it was darker than it should be. Glancing in Lana's direction while still picking up candles, she asked. "What happened to your phone's flashlight?"

At the continued silence, a chill engulfed Mary before she stopped what she was doing and looked at the unnaturally still form in the doorway of the pantry. Mary concentrated on the shape. At the precise second she knew the form in the doorway was too large to be Lana, a voice reached out of the dark and squeezed her heart.

"Marrry!"

∞∞∞∞

"Mary!" Cade shouted into his phone.

Cade's heart thumped in worry as he shouted Mary's name repeatedly, drawing the attention of the state forensic guys who had just arrived and were about to set up lights.

Ignoring the techs, Cade keyed his mic and started running out of the school to his car. "Zebra-12, zebra-12!"

"Zebra-12, go."

"Struthers, what's your twenty?"

"Outside Ms. Smith's house."

"Get in there! Get in there now!"

"Copy, Sheriff."

Cade hopped in his car, turning on lights and a siren. He sped out of the school's parking lot while calling Mary again on his cell. It went directly to voicemail."

"Struthers, you in? Zebra-12?" Cade called over the radio.

Silence. He tried to hail Struthers several more times, all with the same results. No answer.

Swearing, Cade pressed down on the accelerator.

∞∞∞

Mary's scream was cut off by strong hands. One around her throat applied just enough pressure to stop her screaming. The other grabbed one of her breasts as her back was slammed flushed against her intruder's front.

Feeling his erection pushed against her bottom, she struggled harder, pulling at the hand on her throat.

The man easily stopped her struggles, pulling her painfully against his body. Mary's bile rose as he put his face next to hers, cheek to cheek.

He whispered. "Mary, you've been so hard to get alone since your date with that Neanderthal sheriff."

Mary tried kicking his shins, the intruder spun their bodies, slamming her against the shelves. His hand squeezed her breast. He continued in the creepy whisper. "I knew you'd feel so good in my arms."

He thrust his erection against her buttocks—his heavy breathing in her ear. Mary whimpered as he moved his hand on her neck and licked her cheek and the corner of her lips.

 She turned her face away and pushed her hands against the shelves, trying to dislodge his hold on her.

He gave a husky laughed, whispering, "I knew you'd be feisty. Oh, Mary, we're going to be so good together."

Light burst forth suddenly. Mary heard a demand shouted from several feet away. "Let go of the girl and put your hands in the air!"

The intruder kissed Mary on the cheek, squeezing her breast so painfully she saw stars, then she was thrown into the shelves, her forehead striking the third shelf hard. Mary fell to the floor, dazed. Disoriented, she heard a struggle going on, and then a shot rang out before she slipped into oblivion.

∞∞∞

Cade went tearing up Mary's driveway. He shoved the gear into park, leaving the door open. He ran through the wide-open door into the darkened house. On the threshold, he pulled his weapon, pausing to listen. There was only ominous silence. Sweeping his flashlight in a slow arc back and forth, his eyes scanned the foyer. Moving slowly, he made his way down the hall to the living room. There was movement coming from the second entrance into the living room across from Cade as he entered.

"Freeze! Police." Cade shouted, training his light on the newcomer's face. Recognizing Lana, he put his light's beam towards the floor.

"Lana! You okay? Where is Mary?"

Tears streaming down her face, she got out shakily. "I-I-don't know. She went to the k-kitchen. I heard screaming and then a shot. I-it got quiet."

"Okay, come this way and go outside, get in my car, wait there."

Lana quickly followed Cade's orders. Cade continued his search of the house. Upon entering the kitchen, he noticed a flashlight on the floor, its beam casting on the wall. Slowly he advanced to the kitchen center. Looking over the island, he saw the pantry door wide open. Moving his flashlight, he spotted Struthers lying on the floor in the doorway of the pantry.

Rushing over, he checked Struthers for a pulse. Cade felt the steady beat immediately. He quietly called in using the mic on his shoulder, an officer down, backup, and rolled paramedics. Waving his light around the inside of the pantry, the beam caught Mary's sneaker.

Swearing, he went to her. Kneeling again, he checked for her pulse and breathed a sigh of relief when he also felt a less steady beat than Struthers' against his middle and index fingers.

Mary moaned. She felt like she was underwater or many blankets. In her drowsy state, she tried pushing at them. They were suffocating. She needed help. She called out. "M-mike. Mike, help me."

Cade froze at the words coming from Mary. His hand stopped running across her body, looking for obvious injuries. He tried to rouse her again. "Mary, come on, hon, open those beautiful eyes for me."

"Mike." She called out.

Cade frowned. She sounded scared. He recalled his thoughts earlier in the evening when he had been with Mary, wondering if she were a wife or a mother. Could this Mike she called for in her distress be her husband? If so, where the hell was he? Why didn't he respond to any of Cade's official inquiries?

"Mary." He tried again.

Mary swam back to full consciousness. Cade's face waved unsteadily in front of her eyes. "C-Cade?"

"That's right, sweetheart, it's Cade. Come on back to me, sweetie."

"Cade. Oh, Cade." Her voice was more assertive as she tried to sit up.

Cade reached to assist her, putting his gun in his other hand. Just as she opened her eyes fully, there was a click, a burst of light, and then the hum of electricity through the house.

"Boss!" Deputy Boyd shouted.

"Kitchen, Boyd!" Cade answered as he holstered his gun and put a staying hand on Mary's shoulder as she attempted to stand. "Whoa, there. Let's get you checked out before you try anything fancy like standing."

Deputies Boyd and Lockhart entered the kitchen. "Hey, Boss, we checked around the house. It's clear."

Cade took his worried eyes off Mary to spare Boyd a glance. "He's gone." He looked back at Mary, still looking shaken, and then at Struthers, still out cold but breathing. "How we doing with the medic?"

"On the way, Sheriff. Two minutes out." Lockhart answered. "We got Ms. Miles secure in the car."

"Okay, back outside. No one in but the paramedics."

Boyd and Lockhart, giving nods, left the kitchen.

"Cade! He said I was hard to get alone." Mary's voice held stark fear.

He took her in his arms, feeling her tremble. He gently soothed. "Ssh, it's going to be all right. I am not letting him near you again."

Mary held on tight, getting the comfort she needed from Cade's strong arms.

His voice rumbled against her ear through his chest. "Mary, did you see him? Did you recognize his voice?"

Keeping her face on his chest, she shook her head. "No, it was too dark. He stayed behind me. I-I c-couldn't fight him off."

"Ssh, ssh. It's going to be all right." He caressed her back in a gentling motion, giving her reassurances physically and emotionally. He held her until the paramedics arrived.

∞ ∞ ∞

"Sheriff, I'm sorry I dropped the ball," Struthers said, sitting on the E.R. hospital bed.

"It's okay. He must have been in the house already, even when I was there."

"Yeah, but you weren't the one who cleared her house." Struthers was beating himself up over the intruder getting in Mary's house on his watch.

"He could have gotten in after you, and I left. The women were alone for about ten to fifteen minutes."

A doctor came in and checked Struthers out. Cade stood outside waiting for the report on his injuries. After several minutes, the doctor let Cade back in.

"I think we need a cat-scan. Deputy Struthers isn't even sure what he was hit with. Although the skin isn't broken, he's sporting a nice size egg to the side of his head. I am recommending the cat-scan and his being admitted for observation for twenty-four hours."

Cade nodded, knowing the drill. The doctor told Struthers the nurse would be back in just a moment to help him get ready for his cat scan.

"I don't really need to stay, Sheriff. I only have a headache. His admitting me for observations is only a suggestion."

Cade shook his head. "Well, I am making it an order. Get truly back on your feet and cleared medically. You're no good to me if you're not one-hundred percent."

Resigned with his fate, Struthers nodded and then asked, "How is Miss Smith and Miss Miles?"

"Miss Miles was scared but is much better now. I had Lockhart see her home safely. I'm headed back to the other side of the E.R. now. A nurse that specializes in rape kit collection is taking pictures of Miss Smith's injuries."

"Oh, my God! He raped her?" Struthers sat up on the bed. "They were standing, struggling, and fully clothed when I got to them."

"He didn't get to complete the act of rape, thanks to you interrupting him. He got close. He can definitely be charged with a sexual assault."

"Damn." Struthers' expression turned determined. "We'll get 'im Sheriff."

"We will. Right now, you worry about getting and feeling better. I am gonna head over to Miss Smith."

The door to Mary's exam room was just opening as he arrived. The nurse walked out with a couple of sealed bags and a special camera for documenting injuries.

"Hi, Ally. How is she doing?" Ally Martin was one of the best nurses Cade had ever met. He had dated her for about a month when he first arrived, but she ended up with Tim Mendelson. Ending their dating was mutual.

"Hey, Cade. She's shaken, as can be expected. She has early bruising on her left breast, underside, and nipple has a scratch looks like it could be from her attacker's fingernail." Ally shook her head in disgust. "He broke the skin there."

Cade's face turned grim. His anger rose.

Ally held up the camera. "Did you want to see the pictures I took for evidence?"

Cade was about to say yes; after all, he is the sheriff. But an image of Mary's trusting smile and beautiful eyes came to mind. He shook his head no. Mary was the woman he had growing feelings for and was dating. She trusted him. He'd wait. If she felt comfortable enough to show him her injuries herself, he'd look. Otherwise, he'd respect her privacy.

"Can I see her now?"

Ally nodded. "Sure, go right on in. She needs a little reassurance. I haven't seen her looking so tiny, scared, lost, and alone since you brought her to the hospital a year ago."

Nodding, Cade went to Mary's door, giving it a soft rap before opening it.

Mary's eyes grew big at the sight of Cade. Her hands fiddled with the sheet covering her, bringing it up to her neck.

"I thought you were the doctor coming back." Her voice was small.

Cade stopped his progress to her bedside. Pointing a thumb over his shoulder, he said, "I can leave if you're not comfortable with me being here right now."

An emotion shifted behind her eyes, and then her beautiful smile overtook her facial features. She held her hand out. "Of course, I want you here."

Feeling way more relief than he should, Cade returned her smile, closing the space between them and taking her hand in his. He leaned over and kissed her cheek.

"How are you, sweetheart?" Cade sat on the stool that was close to the bed.

Again, he watched emotions move behind her eyes before she asked, "Truth?"

"Always, between us, sweetheart."

"I was so scared, terrified." Her voice held anger.

"Mary, anyone would be scared in your situation."

"Not me!" Mary said with conviction.

Cade's brow furrowed. This wasn't the simple regret of a victim not being able to handle something. "What do you mean?"

"I felt so terrified. That mother fucker had me shaking in my boots like a little girl who got groped for the first time."

Cade tilted his head to the side. His attention was grabbed and centered on the change in Mary's cadence, emphasis, and choice of words. Her voice was stronger than anything he had heard in an entire year. If he had only listened to the voice she was using, he would have assumed it was someone who sounded a little like Mary. He would have never thought it was Mary. Also, she spoke as though she should have handled the situation much better than she did and as someone who had been that little girl that was groped, like she knew deep down what it felt like to be groped for the first time as a little girl. But the one thing that had Cade staring at her in speculation was the fact that she just swore and didn't seem to be aware that she had. She continued to grumble about her inability to fight and handle her attacker better.

Cade gently interrupted Mary's tirade. "Mary?"

She turned a glare on him. Yes, it was an actual glare. "What?" She snapped in an annoyed tone.

Cade's eyebrows rose in surprise. Seeing his expression, she changed hers. It was like a switch was flipped. In a blink of an eye, the sterner, glowering Mary disappeared, and his sweet, shy, Mary was back.

"Uh, Mary, why is it that you think you should have handled the situation better than others?"

"Because I... I...I." Mary's eyes blinked and then widen. "Why?" She asked herself and shook her head in confusion. She looked at Cade with fear in her expression. "That's not right. Is it?" Her hand tightened on his, and her eyes filled with tears and sought his for reassurances.

"Sweetheart, you didn't react any differently than any other victim I have dealt with. There isn't anything right about what you're going through. But there is nothing wrong with your reaction."

She leaned towards him, silently seeking comfort. Cade was more than happy to comply. He pulled her close.

He held her for a few moments in silence. His chin resting on the top of her head and her ear against his chest. Their arms around each other; he said, "Mary, some of what you said sounded as though you were speaking from experience, especially the part about a little girl being groped for the first time."

Mary gasped and leaned back. "Oh, my God. Do you think that's why I feel this way? I am remembering being groped?"

Looking in her eyes, Cade saw her anxiousness over her emotional reaction. He decided to relieve some of the anxiety. "It's possible. I'd say it's highly likely. The doctors did say your memories would come back."

She gave a weak smile. "Thank goodness. I thought I was losing my mind or what there is left of it."

He took her back in his arms. He had left out the part where she just cussed like she was a sailor on leave. Whether they were ready for it or not, it seemed as though Mary's memory was returning. Cade gave her a gentle squeeze, hoping that he wouldn't lose her with her returning memories.

Chapter 6

"Thank you. Have a good day." Mary smiled at the elderly patron.

The library had been busier than usual for the past few days. Most were frequent borrowers, but others Mary had only ever seen somewhere else in town. They were looky-loos. It was human nature to be curious. After three days of people coming up to her and asking if she were okay, Mary was ready for the weekend.

Tonight was Halloween. She was looking forward to handing out candy with Cade. Thoughts of him brought a smile to her lips.

"Such a lovely smile."

Mary's smile widened as she looked at the high school English teacher, Stan Horiwitz. "Hello, Stan. Thank you."

"You're welcome. That smile seemed to have a person behind it." Stan's own smile grew, teasingly he added. "Dare I hope it was I?"

Mary laughed. "It was Cade, of course."

"Of course." Stan feigned shock. "The rest of fellas don't have a chance with him around."

Mary nodded slowly, remembering Stan was one of the men in town that had asked her out. "Without Cade, there would be no me. He saved my life."

Stan bobbed his head in agreement. "He's a good man. Eldred is lucky to have him."

She smiled her agreement. Then asked. "So how can I help this town's most popular teacher?"

Blushing, Stan waved her compliment away. "Nah, I just don't give them a lot of homework. That's why they love me."

Shaking her head, she laughed. "If you heard some of these teenage girls talk about you, you'd know it was more than your lack of homework assignments."

Changing the subject, he asked. "I spoke to Mrs. Hansen about certain reference books I need for class."

Mary turned to get the books with a note on them from her fellow librarian, Mrs. Hansen. "Yeah, they're right here."

Because the library didn't loan out their reference books, there was no barcode to scan into the system as the books being 'out.' But if the local heartthrob high school English teacher couldn't be trusted with the books, then no one could.

Mary put the books in one of the library's tote bags and passed it over the counter to Stan. "Here ya go."

Taking the bag, he gave Mary a big smile. "See you tonight."

Mary's brow lowered. She questioned, "Tonight?"

"The Mayor called a town meeting after school. Cade is going to be there to give his bit on safety."

"Oh, yes, I forgot. See you there."

Stan gave her a final wave before leaving, saying, "It's a date."

Mary had forgotten about the meeting Cade mentioned in passing on one of his visits to check on her after being discharged from the hospital. Since her attack, Cade made sure to always be with her or have one of his men guarding her and her home when he had to be in town. He said the Mayor wanted to get some finer points of the holiday celebration and the charity picnic that wasn't a real picnic as it was being held at the catering hall on the outskirts of town.

Cade said he'd be instituting a curfew for Eldred's Halloween to keep the antics and petty crime down to a minimum. Cade had said most of these crimes were perpetrated by bored teenagers.

Another smile graced her face when her thoughts switch to the other night with Cade.

"So, do you think you're going to like Halloween?" Cade said with a huge grin, taping a jack-o-lantern on Mary's front door.

Mary laughed, strategically placing fake spiders all over the porch. "Why do I get the feeling that it is you who likes it?"

He nodded with boyish enthusiasm. "I admit it. I love the holiday. Ever since my brother and I were little. We'd go all out. My parents too."

"Oh, a brother. There's another of you walking around?" Mary wore a mischievous expression.

Cade's smile disappeared, and he bowed his head. "Not anymore. My brother was killed in a workplace shooting in the city in twenty-nineteen. I hate May twenty-ninth with a passion."

She set the bag of fake spiders down on the porch seat and went to him, hugging him. "I'm so sorry. Was he older?"

He pulled her in his arms and gave a sad smile, "He was two years older. He was my big bro."

"Was he a cop?" Mary looked up at Cade as he stared off in the distance, lost in memories.

"He was a stockbroker, believe it or not."

"Wow. A cop and a stockbroker. That's quite different."

"We were like night and day. It was hard to believe we grew up in the same home with the same parents."

"What's his name?" She placed a soothing hand on his chest.

"Cord," Cade said with reverence.

"That's a nice name." She smiled. "Cord and Cade Myers, huh? Those poor women."

Cade released her and reached for the bag of fake spiders. "Hey, we were perfect gentlemen."

"Uh, huh, sure you were."

Cade laughed. "This is how you decorate for the maximum effect."

He then proceeded to raise the bag of spiders above his head as high as he could reach, then spin with force with the open end of the bag pointing outward. Spiders of all shapes and sizes flew out of the bag, scattering all around them. They fell into each other's arms, laughing.

"I want some of what you had if it's bringing a smile like that to your face." Lana joked.

"It was—"

"Cade. Yes, I know. You guys are joined at the hip." Lana teased her friend, but she was happy for her. "I came by on my break to see if you wanted to go to this town meeting together."

"Yes, that's good. Because I want to go with Cade after the meeting is over, and it would be nice to be in the same car with him instead of him following me home."

"Okay, I'll be at your place at six. The meeting begins at six-thirty. We'll have plenty of time."

"Okay. See you then."

This meeting was turning into a big deal. Mary hoped that everything would go smoothly to give candy out at her house like they planned. Mary dismissed her feelings of unease.

∞∞∞∞

In an angry whisper, Kallie said to Casey, "This is all because of your stupid pranks."

Casey smiled from his position flat on his tummy in the school's auditorium's balcony floor. "Isn't it great?"

"No! It can get us in big trouble."

Casey glared at Kallie. "It can only get us into trouble if you open your fat mouth."

Kallie was hurt by Casey's words. Holding in tears, she countered, "You didn't say anything about my mouth last night."

Casey smirked, putting his index finger against his lips, shushing her.

Kallie rolled her eyes. "Why are we hiding? The meeting is open to us kids too."

Casey nodded his head towards the growing audience and the seats being filled below them. "Do you see any of our classmates down there?"

Kallie took a quick peek. "There's several down there."

Casey whispered, "Yeah, losers and mama boys."

Kallie gave him the side-eye. "Either way. It's stupid to be hiding up here on the balcony, overlooking our friends and family. It's creepy."

"I want to see if Sheriff Myers says anything about that night at the school."

"We could still do that in seats down there."

"Shut up, Kallie. I want to hear."

"There's nothing to hear right now. They're all talking at once. The meeting hasn't started. And we should have gone directly to Sheriff Myers about those guys fighting in the school and that guy killing the other one. It was wrong just to leave."

Casey looked a little guilty. "Billy would have flipped if I were mixed up in something like a dead body. And he'd absolutely lose his shit if he found out I was the one that hurt Principal Simmons. He's constantly going on about our image now that he's a fireman. I never would have been able to give a valid reason for being there."

Kallie peeked down below, spotting Principal Simmons by the podium with a bandage on his hand. She felt guilty just knowing about it and not telling Sheriff Myers. "Still, we should have called the cops." She said.

"Come on, give me a break. We pulled the fire alarm so they could find the body."

"And how do you know he wasn't still alive?"

"Shit, that guy mangled his face and throat. That dude was dust."

Sickened, remembering witnessing one man killing another. It had been her nightmare each night since. The sounds of the struggle, the gurgling sounds the man had made, the awful metallic smell of blood. Kallie shivered. "I still think we should have told Sheriff Myers."

"Well, it's over with now. Besides, what could we have told him? We didn't know those guys or what they were doing there. All we could have said is that they fought, and one guy lost. I think Sheriff Myers is smart enough to have figured that at out all on his own." Putting a finger to his lips again, he added, "Let's hear what he has to say. I want to go back and do what we were going to do that night."

"Oh, no, please, Casey, can't we do something else? Let's go trick-or-treating."

"That's for little kids."

"Then can we please give out candy at my place or yours?"

"No, I want to finish what we started at the school. Besides, we're already here. All we have to do is hide until everyone is gone."

"I have to be home for dinner."

"Then we'll come back later. There's a patrol, so we'll have to wait until late."

Sighing, Kallie gave up trying to convince Casey to do the right thing, looking over the crowd and spotting the Sheriff at the front near the stage with the Mayor and the editor of the Eldred Gazette. She had thoughts of telling Sheriff Myers herself.

"Okay, no more talking. It looks like everyone is here." Casey settled in, looking down through the balcony guardrail.

∞ ∞ ∞

"Whoa!" Lana paused on the threshold of the school's auditorium. She looked over her shoulder at Mary. "I haven't seen this many people in town since old Sheriff Denten had a heart attack."

"Cade and Mayor Bonner made this meeting mandatory for business owners on the main street," Mary said.

They walked in looking for available seats.

"Wow. I don't think we're going to get a seat unless we go to the balcony seating." Lana said, looking around at all the filled seats.

"Look, Cade saved us seats in the front row," Mary said, passing Lana on the aisle, walking into Cade's open arms as he met her halfway.

"Hey, sweetheart." Cade pulled her in close and kissed her forehead.

"Hey. You were not kidding when you said everyone would be here." Mary said, waving a hand at the seated audience.

"I had to make sure the older kids knew that I won't tolerate any funny business tonight and let the parents of younger kids know that it would be safe."

Mary smiled at Cade, full of pride. He was a fantastic sheriff and an even better man.

Cade caught her look, their eyes locked in silent communication.

"Ugh! Being around you two is like being smothered by sugar. I'm going to go sit next to that sexy Stan Horiwitz." Lana laughed.

As if mentioning him somehow brought him closer, he appeared behind Lana. "Did I hear somebody say my name?"

Lana jumped; looking over her shoulder, she said, "I don't see how you could of heard anything in this din."

"That's *could have* not 'could of.'" Stan corrected Lana while looking at Mary. "Hello, Mary, I see you made it. Shall we all find a seat?"

Cade's hand at her waist tightened, causing Mary to look up at him. He was looking at Stan with an odd expression.

"Oh, let's leave these two lovebirds alone," Lana said; turning around, she grabbed Stan's arm. "Come on, Sheriff saved a seat for his girl. I am sure we can find two seats together."

Lana waved her fingers at Mary and Cade and pulled Stan off to find seats.

Mary looked from the retreating couple to Cade, who was frowning after them. "Okay, why the look?"

Cade looked down at Mary. They still had their arms around each other's back. "I didn't know you and Horiwitz were close."

Mary shook her head in confusion. "We're not. I know him from his monthly trips to the library. And he started a reader's group for the high schoolers on Tuesday nights. I see him then occasionally. What makes you think we're close?"

Instead of answering, Cade asked a question of his own. "Wasn't he one of the guys who asked you out?"

Cade wasn't looking at Mary. Following his gaze, Mary spotted Lana and Stan sitting in the last of the seats available. Nodding slowly, "Uh, yes, yes he was."

"What would you say Horiwitz is in height, about five-nine, five-ten?"

"Um, maybe," Mary looked over at Stan again. He was looking at her. When he caught her eye, he smiled and wave. On autopilot, Mary smiled and waved back.

"He certainly acts like you guys are close. I had to turn him away from the hospital."

"What? Why would he go there?"

"My question exactly."

Mary's eyes swung to Cade's. He was still looking at Stan and Lana. She hoped he didn't think she was encouraging Stan.

Before she could say anything, the Principal called the meeting to order. Cade walked her to her seat and took his place next to the mayor at the podium. They first called up Tony Somerville, editor of the Eldred Gazette.

The meeting went smoothly even though the townspeople had many questions. Both the mayor and Cade did a great job of alleviating their fears.

As she listened to Cade explain the curfew for tonight, Mary thought she saw movement peripherally above her.

She turned her head and looked on the balcony. For just seconds, she thought she saw a blond head, but then it disappeared. When the head didn't reappear in her line of vision again, she returned her attention back to the podium. She truly hoped Cade would enjoy this holiday he liked so much with her in peace.

∞∞∞∞

"Trick or Treat!" The kids on Mary's porch yelled.

Laughing, she grabbed the large bowl of candy that sat on a small table in the entryway. Mary made sure she commented on each trick or treater's costume as she dropped some candy in their bags. "Wow, that's an awesome costume! Aww, don't you look cute? Uh, oh, I am scared of you!"

Suddenly, everyone, including the parents with their kids, screamed as Cade came up behind them on the porch, emitting an ominous growl, wielding a sizeable fake butcher knife dressed like the killer from 'Scream.'

When one of the younger girls started to cry and hold on to her father's leg, Cade whipped the mask and hood off, revealing his handsome face.

Her father picked her up, and she buried her face in his chest, crying. Her father soothed her by gently rubbing her back.

Cade soothed too. "Aww, Tina, sweetie, it's okay. It's just me, Sheriff Myers."

The child was instantly relieved when she saw Cade's face. When Cade held out his arms for the child, she happily reached out, allowing Cade to take her out of the shelter of her father's arms. Cade held her with one arm while he tapped her nose. "Sorry about that, honey. Do you forgive Sheriff Myers?" Tina's little head bobbed up and down. She flashed her missing front teeth smile.

"Okay, but you have to give me a peck on the cheek. That way, I know you really forgive me." Tina enthusiastically slapped her hands against Cade's cheeks and gave him a smack on the lips.

Everyone on the porched laughed except Mary. An odd feeling went through her.

She stood stiffly while Cade returned little Tina to her father and spoke to the parents for a few minutes. He put his arm around her waist as he talked. He warned them the curfew was in fifteen minutes, and they all waved goodbye, leaving to their cars parked on the roadside.

Mary turned back into her house, thinking about the strange feeling she got watching Cade kiss little Tina.

"I thought that went great. It was fun." Cade set the bowl down on the little table, closed the door, locking it, and turning off the external lights. "I think next year we should—"

He stopped speaking. Mary was watching him with a look he had only seen one other time, which had been in the hospital when her personality changed.

"Mary?" he asked.

"You shouldn't kiss little girls in the mouth, especially if the child isn't yours. It's inappropriate."

Her tone and diction were also from when she was in the hospital bed.

"Her father was right there." Cade's brows lowered.

"It's inappropriate no matter who is around." Mary reiterated more forcefully.

Baffled, Cade wondered what she was saying. Was she accusing him of something? "I said cheek, and she planted one on my mouth. It's no big deal. She's a kid, practically still a baby."

"It is a big deal. She's a kid, and you're an adult who should have stopped her unless that's what you wanted. It's disgusting and inappropriate, Mike." Mary shouted and turned and walked away, speaking angrily under her breath.

Cade was shocked and pissed. Did she just accuse him of being a pedophile? But, more importantly, did she realize she just called him by another man's name?

Chapter 7

Cade tried to keep his rising anger down. He followed her to the kitchen. She was clearing the empty trays that had held the cupcakes they had given out to the earlier trick-or-treaters. They were delicious and had gone fast. Cade had eaten three himself.

Mary put the trays into the dishwasher, slamming the dishwasher door and using far more strength than necessary to push the buttons to start the cycle.

"Just what are you getting at, Mary?" Cade walked to her, blocking her from leaving the kitchen.

"It isn't right," Mary said with a less aggressive tone.

"I've known little Tina since I arrived in Eldred. Her parents are good people that have had me over to their place several times. I've been with all their kids, who happen to be all daughters, ranging in ages of three to fourteen, which they are now four to fifteen. I've even been alone with the girls when their parents needed to leave overnight on an emergency. So, what exactly are you saying isn't right?"

She started strong. "It isn't right for a grown man to... to...t..." Mary's words trickled to a stop. She blinked, and then she was the sweet Mary he'd known for over a year. Her eyes widen in fear. A trembling hand touched her forehead. "Oh my God. What's happening to me?"

Feeling her confusion and fear from the few feet that separated them, he pulled her into his arms. He was relieved when she clung to him and laid her head on his chest. He put gentle kisses on each side of her temple and the top of her head. "I think it's safe to say your memories are colliding with present day. They're catching up to you in the here and now."

"I am scared. Maybe I don't want the memories back. What if I am someone no one likes or a mean person?"

Cade laughed out loud. "Oh, sweetheart, I can guarantee you're not someone anyone could dislike. You practically have the entire town wrapped around your finger."

Mary leaned back to catch Cade's eyes. "I am afraid to find out, but I need to know who I am. Is there something else we can do to find out who I was?"

Cade's brow furrowed. He didn't like that she was referring to herself in the past tense. He didn't want to bring up the name she had called him either. She seemed fragile at this moment. However, he had done absolutely everything legally there was to do to find out Mary's identity. Thinking of a former classmate and former fellow NYPD detective in the FBI, perhaps there was something else he could do.

"I have another avenue I can try. Which I will do as soon as I return to the station. I also think we should bring Doc Murrow back into your life. Maybe he can help you with these bouts of memories that are being triggered."

"Yes, I think that's a great idea." Mary smiled the smile Cade was used to seeing aimed his way.

"What do you say about continuing our night?" He suggested.

Mary's smile turned playful, "I'd love that. Go into the living room. I have a surprise for you."

Cade tipped his head to the side. "Where are you going?"

She bit the corner of her lip and looked at him through a veil of lashes. Cade felt his dick twitch in his pants. She was so gorgeous but also shy. "I thought I'd go slip into something more comfortable."

Her eyes were warm and inviting. They conveyed something sweet, sexy, hot! Cade swallowed. He nodded. "I'll lock up and meet you in the living room."

She smiled excitedly and almost ran towards the stairs. Cade locked the back door and checked all windows on the first floor and the window in the laundry room beyond the mudroom near the back door. As he closed shades, locked windows, turned off lights, Cade realized this house was entirely too expensive for a librarian's salary. How did Mary afford this house?

When Mary was healed enough to be discharged from the hospital, there weren't too many places she could have gone. The state facility about an hour away was suggested by Dr. Murrow. Mary had balked at the idea, saying she didn't want to leave, literally, the only place she knew.

Cade had been ready to take her home to his place even though he felt it would conflict since he was working her case. Tony Somerville, the editor for the Eldred Gazette, had been at the hospital to take pictures of Mary to get her 'Do You Know Her' story out. He had overheard Mary's dilemma and had offered his rental property. The house was a four-bedroom that was modernized with all the amenities; washer, dryer, stainless steel appliances, large kitchen island with a mini-fridge and wine rack attached, fireplaces in the living room, and the upstairs master bedroom, which had an en-suite bathroom. The furnishings were on the high end of expensive. Making his way to the living room, he decided to ask Mary when she returned from upstairs how she could afford a house such as this with a librarian's salary.

Upon entering the living room, Cade froze, looking around. Mary had lit a small fire in the fireplace, had popcorn in a huge bowl, several chocolate bars from the Halloween candy they had bought, and cans of root beer soda, his favorite. There were rolled sleeping bags and pillows alongside the fireplace in perfect alignment with the sixty-inch smart tv. Mary had remembered one of his most favorite memories from childhood that he had shared with her. She had recreated it for him. He was touched. He smiled.

"Did I get it right?" softly spoken from behind him.

Cade turned. "It's per—" His words caught in his throat at the vision that met his eyes.

Mary wore her hair down, a rare thing. She always wore her librarian bun. Now its thick volume fell a bit past her shoulders in jet black waves. A simple white silk nightgown clung to her curves, accentuating them in alluring subtlety. Her nipples pushed at the delicate silk. Her cute toes peeked out from the bottom with a French pedicure that matched her hands. The spaghetti straps were thin wisps on her sexy shoulders. With that thought, Cade knew he was a goner. *He thought her shoulders were sexy.* He had never thought any other woman's shoulders were sexy. He thought everything about Mary was sexy. Shit, her breathing was sexy to him.

Mary's breath came out in measured intakes and exhales as she saw the appreciation and hunger in Cade's eyes. She got nervous when all he did was continued to stare. Then she wasn't sure if his look meant what she thought. She blurted the first thing that came to her mind. "Lana did it."

Cade chuckled and came to her. "Well, remind me to thank that meddling woman."

"So, you *do* like it?" Mary's question held relief.

He cupped her silky shoulders, caressing them softly. All the mirth left his gaze as it hooked hers. Then he said with seriousness, "I love it."

His words conveyed more than the approval of her wardrobe change. He lowered his head, and she went on her toes. Their mouths touched. They both moan at the same time. Cade lapped at her lips until she gasped sexily and opened her mouth in invitation. Cade thrust his tongue inside, rubbing along hers as he tasted his fill.

"Mmm, baby, I love this too." He pulled her flushed against him so that she could feel the bulge she created.

She groaned. "Cade, I want to share tonight with you and experience one of your great memories of Halloween."

He nodded. "Why don't you get settled by the fire while *I* go change into something more comfortable." He smiled suggestively.

Mary picked up the sleeping bags, attaching them via their zippers. She spread them out and threw the blankets over them. She grabbed up the remote from the coffee table and turned on the tv. She had her streaming program up with a playlist of three horror movies. She lit strategically placed candles and turned off the overhead light and lamp. She had just placed the pillows when Cade returned.

She gasped, staring at Cade in only his boxer briefs. Mary had known Cade had a nice body underneath his uniform. But nothing prepared her for the reality of what his uniform only hinted at. Cade was gorgeous, from his rippling muscled abs to his enormous pecs. His chest was hairless, revealing every single delicious muscle. He strode to her with his masculine gait, smiling.

"A guy could get used to this."

On autopilot, Mary brought her hand up and placed it on his impressive pec. "So could a gal."

Cade pulled her into his arms. She went happily. They kissed, deep, sharing kisses, taking turns, bringing each other to intense heat. Their tongues swirled around each other's until they needed air.

Cade scooped her up in arms. Mary gave a startled yelp, reaching for his shoulders. He placed her in the center of the makeshift bed, moving in close, lying alongside her, the front of his body flushed to her side.

He cupped her cheek, staring into her dark brown orbs that had gotten even darker since they started kissing. "Mary, you're so beautiful."

Her hand came up and brushed back a lock of his hair that had fallen on his forehead. "You're not so bad yourself, Sheriff."

"Keep talking like that, and I don't think we'll get to the horror movies." He teased.

"Oh, is that supposed to scare me?" Mary's eyes danced with laughter.

His eyes grew serious; he pushed her hair off her shoulder and slipped his hand under the strap of her gown. Moving his hand slowly, he whispered, "It scares me how much I want you. I've never wanted a woman like I want you."

Shivers ran down her body as his big, calloused hand moved over her shoulder and down her arm, pulling the nightgown down on one side, exposing her breast.

Seeing the bruises left by her attacker caused his expression to turn grim, his jaw clenched in anger. "When I catch that motherfucker, I'll break his God damn arm."

Automatically Mary placed a finger over his lips. "Don't cuss."

Cade smiled, moving the finger across his lips. He leaned over her breast while hovering mere centimeters above her nipple; he husked out, "You're right. I can think of better things to be doing with my mouth."

His tongue struck out, giving the tip of her nipple three rapid flicks. She cried out in shock, squirmed her body closer to his, and parted her legs. Mary's reaction made Cade's cock grow. He moaned and repeatedly circled his tongue around her hardening nipple.

Mary's vocals increased as her hands threaded through the hair at the back of his head. She arched sharply, pushing his head closer to her nipple.

Cade growled and pulled her nipple entirely into his mouth, drawing on it like it was his lifeline. He suckled on her breast for several moments alternating between licking the crest and sucking the now hard bud into his mouth, giving it gentle bites, her moans, and groans feeding his need for her.

"Oh, God! I think something is ha-happening. Oh, oh, oh!"

Cade heard the slight fear of the unknown, the shock and the surprising pleasure in Mary's tone. He released her nipple. Ignoring her cry of frustration, he exposed her other breast. Pulling up the bottom of her nightgown to her waist, exposing her womanhood, his hand cupped her mons. He felt her heat and wetness from the tame touch. He licked the underside of both breasts, and then on the newly exposed one, he licked in concentric circles until the tip of his tongue was flicking the tip of her nipple.

Mary cried out in pleasure. "Oh!"

Cade's fingers swiped her stripe of hair before gently parting her nether lips. His fingers played in the wetness he found there. Teasing her labia before sliding a finger insider her pussy.

Mary arched deeply, her back leaving the floor. "Cade, oh, Cade!"

He suckled her breast, added a finger sliding in and out of her pussy, and put his thumb on her engorged clit, stroking in concert with sucking on her breasts.

Mary screamed, squirmed, and blindly grabbed onto his bicep. "Oh, Cade, it's happening. Oh, God!"

Cade smiled against her breast in male pride. She sounded shocked but also beyond pleased. He released her nipple speeding up his to and fro inside her and his unrelenting tweaking of her clit. He looked at her pussy, watched his fingers disappear inside her. His cock grew impossibly hard. Her panting increased. Her legs trembled uncontrollably.

His name fell from her lips almost piously. "Cade, Cade! Oh, Cade!"

"That's it, baby, give it to me. Show me how much you like this!"

As if her body was attuned to his command, Mary gave a loud shout, and her legs tightened up just as her pussy gripped his fingers, and then she started coming, which turned surprisingly into Mary squirting. The stream shot out as Cade continued the motion of his hand. Her whole body shook as he continued to move his hand, slowing it down as her pussy's grip on his fingers loosened. She collapsed on the sleeping bag, drained.

Cade smiled and winked as she looked at him in awe. Her eyes searched his face in wonder. He said cockily. "Another new?"

Her head bobbed as she still caught her breath. "I'll say. That felt amazing."

Cade stood and pulled off his boxer-briefs, freeing his thick, long cock. "It gets better."

Mary's eyes widen at his words and at his body. "Oh, my. I've seen one in books, and I read a bit about the penis in the anatomy books, but boy, nothing beats reality."

Cade laughed. "You read about the penis?"

"Of course, I read about my vagina too. But, like I said, nothing beats reality. For some reason, the human anatomy didn't survive my memory loss."

He held his cock in his hand, lifting it up, giving her a profile of it, and lifted it again so she could see his balls. "Well, do I measure up to the pictures and the information you read?"

Mary sat up, so his cock was eye level. She shook her head, grasping his dick. "No, you exceed it."

It was Cade's turn to gasp and groan. Mary's hand fisted his cock, sliding down to the base of his shaft and stroking back up to his tip, with her palm, picking up the precum coming from his head and then stroking back down.

"Mmm, shit, that feels good, baby."

Mary stared up at Cade. His body was incredible. His skin unmarred, his face had no lines in them. His cock in her hand felt strong and vital. While still stroking his cock, Mary asked, "Cade?"

He had thrown his head back and closed his eyes. He opened them and looked down at Mary, focusing on what her hand was doing to his body. "Hmm?"

"How old are you?"

In a daze, he answered while still watching Mary's hand on his cock. "I'll be thirty-six on January fifteenth."

She gave his dick a couple more strokes before she lowered her hand and looked at him with such a sad look and asked, "How old do you think I am?"

Cade sat next to her, hugging her. "Oh, baby. I am so sorry this happened to you. I don't always realize how traumatizing your situation truly is, and I am sorry for that too."

"It's alright. I understand. It's a strange position to be in. I don't always know how deep my issue is until I am confronted with certain things. You should have seen me the first day I was in this home alone and walked past a mirror. I freaked for several seconds because I didn't recognize my own reflection. I thought my reflection was an intruder."

"Wow, I didn't even think about that."

Mary shook her head. "Ugh, look at me, bringing down the mood like the Hindenburg. I am sorry."

Cade tilted his head. "See, that's the part I don't get about your condition."

Mary frowned. "What?"

"You can remember a part of history, but you can't remember what you look like? Or the human anatomy."

She nodded. "Dr. Murrow says it's retrograde amnesia and dissociative amnesia. I can't remember my past, any specifics regarding me or the attack which caused me to have amnesia."

"I think you should definitely see Dr. Murrow again. I'd feel better knowing he's helping you through this part of your healing. You have obviously been experiencing some form of memory recovery."

She looked deeply into his eyes. "Cade, I am scared."

"Don't be. I'll be here with you every step of the way. Always where you are. Always."

She smiled and looked down his body at his semi-hard cock. "I see I haven't totally ruined the mood for you."

Cade chuckled. "That's not happening with your gorgeous body, not even a foot from me."

She initiated a kiss. Cade quickly took over. While he kissed her, he laid her back down, following with his body next to hers. She lay on her back, looking up at him. He looked down at her, supporting himself with one hand while his other stroked a finger along her delicate jawline.

"Hmm, let's see. You have smooth, wrinkle-free skin." He picked up a strand of her hair. "Your hair is thick and lustrous, healthy." His hand moved, trailing a caress along her neck.

He whispered, "Your skin is also soft, supple." He continued his caress downward. As he kissed the side of her neck, she lifted her chin, giving him greater access. "Mmm, you smell incredible."

He gently took hold of her breast. "Your breasts are soft like pillows yet firm, your nipples are medium size, and the areola about the size of a quarter. I have it on good authority women's areolas tend to increase in circumference with each childbirth and age."

He licked the object of his observation. Mary moaned and grabbed the back of his head, holding him there.

Cade gave her breast one last lick before continuing. "Your belly is flat, your hips sexily curved." He kissed and licked her belly, his tongue circling her inny belly button before licking a hot trail to her hip. He licked and kissed her there.

Cade maneuvered until he was positioned between her thighs, removing her nightgown from around her waist and tossing it over his shoulder. Assisting with removing the gown, Mary raised her hips and then widened her legs to make room for him, trembling.

"Mm, this little landing stripe on your pussy is a habit of younger age groups." His tongue swiped down the stripe. Then his fingers gently parted her lips, he licked her from gate to clit. "Mm, your pussy is juicy, wet, hot." He dipped a finger inside her and licked her clit.

Mary began to pant and writher. "Oh, Cade!"

"Mm, look who came out to play. Your clit is swollen and pushing out of her hiding place." He sucked her clit before giving it a tiny bite and then soothing it with languid strokes of his tongue.

"Oh, God, it's happening again!"

Cade lifted up, positioning himself between her legs. He took his cock in his hand as Mary gapped her legs. He put the head of his penis at her entrance, and he paused, looking into her eyes. "Baby, are you sure? I don't think I'll be able to stop once I'm in. It's been a while for me too."

Trailing her fingers down his chest to his washboard abs, she blew out a breath, nodding vigorously. "Yes, Cade. Please."

He smiled and switched his gaze to the point where their genitals met. He pushed in an inch. Mary gasped loudly, and he groaned.

He pushed in slowly, feeling her walls clutch at his shaft. "Fuck, fuck! It's so good."

Instinctively Mary began thrusting her hips, keening out unintelligible words. Cade swore and gripped her hips. "No, baby, slow down."

"I don't want to, please, Cade."

Cade's jaw was clenched tight in restraint; sweat popped onto his forehead as he held back from slamming into Mary and going full blast.

"Baby, I need to go slow with you. Please stop moving!" He said through gritted teeth.

"Please, now, now!"

Looking at her face beautifully distorted in pleasure, her biting her lip, pulling at the blanket and, her bouncing breasts from her trying to dislodge his hold on her hips so she could thrust was all too much for Cade. He released her hips and planted his palms flat on the floor, holding himself above her. He then followed his male instinct, slamming into Mary to the hilt.

She cried out. While he slipped into heaven, he looked at her face to make sure she wasn't hurt. "Mary, baby, you, okay?" He panted as he started long stroking.

"Oh, yes, Cade!" she panted in return, grabbing onto his arms, wrapping her legs around his waist.

He felt the vibrations of the clutching and release of her walls on his cock. "Mm, damn, baby, yes, just like that!"

Mary's head thrashed on the pillows. She swirled her hips, and Cade became a piston as he felt the onset of her orgasm. He power-drove his cock into her pussy.

Mary cried out in immense pleasure. His thick long cock filled her. Hitting areas inside Mary didn't know existed. Her nails scored his arms as she began to come hard. She screamed, holding on to his arms.

Cade growled and pumped inside Mary three more times and then held deep inside her as his cock release his load. She was still twitching and jerking from her own orgasm.

He was pouring sweat. He blew out a breath, leaning over he touched their foreheads together. They gazed deeply into each other's eyes. They smiled simultaneously and said together, "Wow!"

Chapter 8

Cade slowly pulled out of Mary. They both groaned. Even pulling out of her felt good. He rolled to the side of her. Feeling the wetness, he winced a little.

"We've made a mess." He laughed.

Mary chuckled. "I didn't feel it until this very moment. I think I made most of the mess."

Cade waggled his eyebrows. "You're welcome."

Mary laughed and playfully slapped his bicep. "So, cocky."

He shook his head and winked at her. Then he tilted his head. "Based on your body, I'd say you are in your twenties. But based on the way you carry yourself. I'd say the early thirties."

"Do you think I am younger or older than you?"

His eyes squinted in scrutiny. "Your body has a feminine tone and tightness." He wagged his eyebrows at her again. "And, I do mean tight, outside and *inside*. You're probably younger than me."

Mary smiled and bowed her head. "You liked it? Me?"

Cade leaned over and kissed her. "Baby, I *loved* our sex." He kissed her and then playfully swatted her backside when she turned into the kiss. "Face it, Mary Smith, you're a hottie."

Mary laughed then suggested, "Let's clean up, remake the 'bed' and continue with our night."

"Sounds like a plan."

They stood and started for the stairs. Mary hesitated. She paused and turned to Cade. "Do you want to shower together, or would you prefer to use the guest bathroom."

"Mary, of course, I want to be where you are." He paused, his look turning serious as he cupped her cheek and held her gaze; he whispered, "Always, where you are. Always."

He lowered his head and kissed her lovingly.

Satisfied, Mary smiled when the kiss ended and grabbed his hand and ran upstairs with him.

It didn't hit her until she was standing in her bathroom and starting the shower that she had just strutted through her house completely naked. Since she woke in the hospital, she had made sure she was covered head to toe. She shook her head, amazing the things you'll do when you feel secure.

"What's that look?" Cade asked.

She looked up into the mirror. Cade was standing behind her, but he must have seen her expression via the mirror. She took in their image. They looked good together. A perfect contrast. Him masculine, her feminine. Him white, her black. They made a striking couple.

"Hey, now, what's *that* look?" Cade asked while holding her gaze in the mirror.

She shook her head. "It's nothing. I was just thinking about how secure I feel when I am around you and with you. I feel like I can do anything with you. The fear I've felt since I woke up in that hospital goes away when I am with you."

He hugged her to him from behind. The bathroom was steamy from the shower she started. He held her eyes through the mist. "Mary, you never have to be afraid with me. Never."

She turned in his arms and wrapped her arms around his neck, bringing his head down for a kiss. While they kissed, Cade lifted her. Instinctively she wrapped her legs around him. He stepped into the shower.

They took turns washing each other, gliding soapy hands over sleek bodies. The only sounds heard were their gasping breaths, moans, and groans. As they were rinsing off, Cade turned Mary to face him. He pulled her flushed against his body, fitting them together like puzzle pieces with his hands on her ass cheeks, caressing in a circular motion.

"Mary, you trust me, yes?"

The water hitting the sides of their bodies, the steam swirling around them. Her hands were on his shoulders. "Of course, I do."

He raised his eyebrows. "Want to try another new?"

His look was mischievous and sexy with a hint of lust. Mary nodded. "Yes, I want to try another new."

He turned her, so they were no longer standing in the stream of the shower. He had her face the shower wall. Taking her hands, he raised them above her head and placed them flat against the tiles. He moved in close behind her.

Mary's breath caught as she felt his dick harden and rise against her back and butt. He glided his hands down her arms, tickling her pits before moving on to cup her breasts.

He gave her behind a swat and whispered in her ear, "Stick your spectacular ass out, and don't take your hands off that wall."

Mary's pussy clenched, and she became wetter at his command. She took in a deep breath and prepared for anything. She gave a tiny yelp when Cade parted her butt cheeks and smeared some shower gel all along her crack. He then massaged her cheeks in a rhythmic caress. Kneading her cheeks, his tongue made a trail on the back of her neck to her other ear.

"I've been dreaming about this ass since you got out of the hospital." He paused his massage to give each cheek a pat and then part them, exposing her anus. "Mmm, look at that."

He tongued her ear then whispered. "Tell me you want me here." His finger circled her puckered hole.

Mary moaned and pushed her ass out further, silently begging for more. He swatted her ass again and started to slowly push a thumb into her anus. "I want to hear you say it. Say you want my cock inside you, in this delicious ass."

"I want it! I want your cock in my ass!" Mary screamed out.

Cade reached around and plucked her clit, and stroked her labia. "Come on, baby, widen your legs."

Mary complied and felt the blunt tip of his cock at her pussy's entrance. His hand left her clit and reached for her breast. Nimble fingers finessed her nipple as he thrust into her pussy.

Upon his entrance, Mary was lifted onto her toes. He felt incredible inside her, filling her to capacity. Her pussy's walls greedily clenched and clamped onto his dick. She tried to keep up with his thrusting, but it got too fast for her, and the pleasure was too intense to concentrate on anything else but keeping her hands against the wall, breathing, and enjoying his slick thrusts.

Cade felt the telltale signs of Mary's orgasm. He gave another twirl of his cock and thrust and then pulled out right before Mary could come. She slapped the tiles in frustration and gave a holler of disappointment. His hands grabbed her hips, keeping one anchored on her hip. Cade used his other hand to slowly feed his cock into Mary's ass.

Mary hissed at the slight sting and pinch as his dick pushed further inside her ass. She inched up more on her toes. Then she felt his touch on her clit again, distracting her from the pinching pain as he pushed past her sphincter muscles. As he completely filled her up, his groan was on the back of her neck as he started to pump into her in earnest.

"So, fucking good! Damn, baby," Cade panted out as he pumped and played with her nipple with one hand and her clit with the other.

Mary's nipples ached deliciously, and her clit was engorged with pleasure. She felt her pussy gush as Cade sped up his thrusts. She screamed as a delightful wave washed over her entire body, and her muscles all tightened in rapture.

When Mary's muscles tightened on his cock, Cade was a goner. His balls tightened up, and his sperm came rushing to the tip of his cock, spewing into her ass.

They both shook uncontrollably. Cade was holding Mary up, for she lost all ability to stand. He leaned against the shower wall holding her tight, taking deep breaths to regain control. After a moment of leaning, he rewashed them both.

He turned the water off and helped Mary to dry off. They gathered new linens and returned to the living room. They quickly remade their 'bed,' and Cade ran the soiled linens to the hamper in the laundry room.

When he returned, he paused on the threshold of the living room. The soft glow of the fireplace caught Mary's body just right. She was an exceptionally beautiful woman. The light glanced off her full globes and sexy curves. He smiled. Her hair turned into a puffy mess after she towel-dried it. She had wanted to blow dry it into straight tresses. Cade told her he wanted her in his arms all-naturel. She had to be convinced, finally giving in when he told her she could be bald, and he'd still want her. His dick wouldn't get any less hard. She was pointing the remote at the tv. She started the first horror movie.

"Starting without me?" He said from where he stood.

Mary turned with a smile. "No, I was going to pause at the beginning of the credits."

Her smile widened as she looked at him standing in the archway, his arms crossed against his chest, watching her. Her eyes travel down from his brunette head to his large feet. He was beyond sexy. He was the epitome of a woman's fantasy lover.

He cocked a brow. "Like what you see?" He walked to her, stopping directly in front of her.

Her eyelashes lowered shyly, and she bowed her head. He used a finger to tip it back up. "You don't have to be shy with me. Besides, women aren't the only ones to appreciate a compliment every now and then. A man likes to know his woman likes his body."

Mary flashed perfectly straight white teeth then put her arms around his neck. His hands went automatically to her waist. "I'm your woman now?" She grinned and added, "Well, Sheriff Myers, I love what I see very much."

His hands slid to her ass. Gripping her cheeks, he lowered his head for a kiss, whispering just before their mouths touched, "Good because Sheriff Myers loves what he sees when he looks at you. And damn skippy, you're my woman now." He kissed her fiercely, leaving no doubt to whom she belonged.

Mary moaned, holding on with her hands at his nape. Breathless, she pulled back to look into his eyes. "I'm good with that."

"Let's lie down and watch these movies," Cade suggested.

Mary nodded her head. She pulled back the fresh blanket and sat down. She looked up and watched Cade grab a towel from the sofa he had brought with them after their shower. He sat next to her, placing the towel by the pillows.

With raised brows, she asked, "What's the towel for."

Cade's expression was cocky again. Mary wasn't sure whether she liked that look yet. However, it made her smile when he did it.

"My woman tends to squirt when we're loving." Cade's tone was full of male pride.

Mary slapped a hand to her forehead. "Oh, my God, that was so embarrassing."

Cade chortled. "Yeah, ah, no. That was fucking awesome!"

Automatically she placed a finger across his lips. "Don't cuss."

Cade moved her hand off his lips and laughed out loud, reminding her, "You didn't seem to mind my language when I was balls deep in that yummy pussy."

She slapped his arm playfully. "Oh, my God! I mean it, Cade, you better not ever mention that to *anyone*."

His eyes popped. "Are you kidding me? Why would I tell competition that my woman comes like crazy and squirts?"

Her brow furrowed. "What competition?"

"Uh, let's count, shall we. We have our friendly neighborhood fireman who thinks he has sole rights to you because you guys are black. There's the nerdy English teacher, Horiwitz, who drools over you every time he sees you. Then there is Tony Somerville who is so besotted with you he lets you live in this four-bedroom, all the amenities, furnished, luxury home for free!"

Mary's spine stiffened in rejection of his words. "*I do not live here for free*. Tony let me stay here for free when I first got out of the hospital because I had nowhere to go. He was just being nice and a good community leader. He is one, you know. He's just as popular as you and the Mayor. And as soon as I got the job at the library, I started paying Tony rent."

Cade shook his head. "Mary, with your salary, there is no way you'd be able to afford a place like this without a mortgage or a seriously reduced rental fee."

"What are you saying?" Mary was starting to get upset.

"All I am saying is that Somerville is hot for your bod so much he doesn't care about profit. He's about five-nine, five-ten and slender in build."

Mary bit her lip nervously. "You said that about Stan at the meeting. What does that mean?"

Cade looked at her, pausing, not sure he wanted to turn their night too serious. Sighing, he told her the truth. "The guy I chased out of the library and attacked you in your kitchen is slender in build and is about five-nine, five-ten in height."

Mary's facial features crumpled into fear. "Oh, no."

Cade took her in his arms. "Baby, I won't let him hurt you ever again. I promise."

Mary leaned back, looking into Cade's unwavering gaze. She believed him. She laid her head on his chest, hugging him tightly. "Thank you for being here with me through all of this."

He stroked her back with his chin on the top of her head. "Always where you are, always."

They settled down in the pillows, sleeping bags, and blankets. The only light in the room coming from the fireplace and the tv. As she laid in the comfort of Cade's arms, she thought about all he had to deal with as the Sheriff. She lazily caressed his chest and abdomen, kissing his pec, and asked, "You must be terribly stressed with all that's going on in town."

He sighed heavily. "I'm holding it all together. But sometimes it feels like I haven't left the big city. Perhaps I didn't get further enough away."

"Besides my stalker, I know you're looking for Mandy, and now that body that was found at the school. What else?"

Cade looked at her tucked so trustingly against him. He had been about to give her his rote answer that he couldn't discuss active cases he had given girlfriends in the past. Instead, he decided to give her some of the trust she gave him.

"I have a missing, a prankster, a stalker, a murderer and partridge in a pear tree, fa, la, la, la, fucked." He sang off-key.

Mary reached her hand up, touching his lips. "Don't cuss."

Cade rolled his eyes, knowing she couldn't see him in her position against his chest. "I'll try not to around you." He sighed and continued. "I haven't a clue of the red x prankster's identity. All I can say is, I'd bet my paycheck that it's a local kid. No one in town has seen Mandy Odessa since she left for her staycation. I think your stalker is one of the guys that asked you out, and I have no idea whatsoever who the killer is because I have no idea who the victim is. All I know about him is he isn't local. Waiting for all the lab and forensic reports," Cade decided to leave out the possible hitman headed to Eldred.

Mary looked up at Cade. "How do you know that he isn't local?"

Cade had a sheepish look on his face. "Honey, when you arrived in town, you brought our African American populous to a whopping three. You, Madson, and old Arlo, who owns the gas station in town. The dead guy is neither, but he is black. Madson had one thing right, there aren't enough blacks in the dating pool in Eldred."

"I can't believe all you're dealing with." Mary thought about whether she could help him with his caseload in any way possible. "Well, Mandy may not be missing at all. She loves those hiking trails and woods. She spends hours up there; hiking, camping, and enjoying nature."

"I knew she liked the outdoors, but I had no idea she was *that* into it."

"Oh, she's nuts for it. You know she's a prepper. She has a go-bag and everything. One day when I was at her house, she showed me everything she has packed in it. She even has tools to purify water, build a fire without matches or a lighter. She has this emergency blanket for hypothermia that folds up to a square that fits in her palm."

"Do you have a way into Mandy's place?"

"Yes, I know where she keeps her hide-a-key."

"We'll go by her place and see if her prepper's go-bag is missing too."

Cade tightened his arms on Mary. "Let's get this movie fest started."

Mary snuggled closer, trying not to yawn.

Cade smiled and pressed play. He took the towel and put it to the side.

Mary did yawn. "You were optimistic, thinking we'd have sex a third time."

Cade kissed her. He made it a hot, deeply arousing kiss. He pulled back and laughed, flicking one of her hardened nipples. "Optimistic, huh?"

She pushed his hand away and snuggled to him. "Oh, shut up."

Cade laughed and pulled her close as he began to watch the movie. He held Mary all through the first movie. She hadn't lasted more than fifteen minutes when he heard her slight snore.

As the second movie started, he changed their positions into a spooning one, careful not to wake her.

They slept together comfortably for a couple of hours when Cade awoke to Mary's distress.

She was moving against his arm around her, thrashing her legs. Her head moved across the pillow in agitation. At first, he couldn't understand the words she mumbled, but they became clearer.

"Mike. Mike, help me. Please, Mike, where are you?" Her pleas were pitiful. She sounded scared.

Cade moved in close, soothing her agitation. He aligned their bodies, putting her buttocks against his crotch and his chest to her back. He gently rocked her, kissing her cheek.

He whispered softly in her ear. "Ssh, Mary, baby, it's okay. I'm here."

He kissed her cheek again, and she settled down. Then a small smile graced her lips. Then she said, "Cade" in a far happier voice.

Cade couldn't stop the smile on his face or his cock from responding. He made love to Mary from behind. She gasped, moaned, called out his name in pleasure several times, and then climaxed. Cade didn't think she awoke completely at all.

After he exploded inside her, satisfied that she knew who was fucking her even in sleep. He cuddled close. He remained deep inside her until his cock grew flaccid and slipped from her pussy's grasp. Then he was the one snoring.

∞∞∞∞

"Seriously, Casey!" Kallie glared as she held the flashlight to the side door of their high school, which led to the gym and pool areas.

"Man, you whine a lot."

"It's fucking freezing out here. You said I couldn't wear my coat again. This hoodie isn't enough. And it's after two-thirty in the morning."

"Sssh! We had to wait until that extra patrol Sheriff Myers put on the school to do it's the last pass through."

"Why do you know so much about what the cops are doing?" Kallie moved her feet to get some warmth.

"My brother Billy talks a lot. He's sweet on one of the weekend dispatchers."

"I thought your brother was dating Miss Odessa."

"He is." Casey gave a purely masculine laugh.

Kallie shoved him in his back. "Hurry up!"

"Be quiet. I almost got it." With those words, he looked over his shoulder and stuck out his tongue. "Ha! Told you I'd get it."

"Where did you learn to do tha—" Kallie had second thoughts; holding up a hand, she said instead, "Never mind. I don't even want to know."

"Come on," Casey said, picking up two of the containers they brought, leaving two for Kallie.

Kallie gave a long-suffering sigh and picked up the remaining containers, following Casey inside.

Once they were inside, it went quickly. They clogged the filters and dumped the large container of dark red paint in the pool. Kallie went to the main office and poured a trail of red paint all over the office and in the hallway leading to it. Casey hadn't told her where he was going with the other two containers --and she really didn't care-- only to meet him back at the door when she was done with her *assignment*. She just wanted to get out of there. She walked past the guidance office where they had witnessed the man murdered. Kallie shivered and picked up her pace, heading back to the door they entered.

She was standing alone in the darkened pool area, wondering why she was letting Casey get away with all this silly prank stuff. They've been dating since before the Halloween dance. It turned out that he wasn't totally one-track-minded. Kallie had a lot of fun at the dance. Casey kept his attention on her the whole evening. He even had a make-out session with her that made her feel special and grown-up. He had his good moments. He wasn't so ba—

The sudden sound of fast-moving footsteps caused Kallie to look toward the doorway. They were headed her way, fast running feet. She hoped it was Casey. She had a tense few seconds, and he appeared running through the doorway.

Kallie didn't know why she whispered. They were the only fools here. "Why are you running?"

Casey merely smiled, pulled the fire alarm next to the door, and ran outside. Kallie screamed out in annoyance and quickly followed Casey.

Chapter 9

Cade bolted upright at the persistent buzzing of his phone and his radio crackling to life.

"Dispatch to Sheriff Myers, come back."

Cade stopped his phone from buzzing, looking over at Mary. He answered his radio while winking at Mary and blowing her a kiss as she slowly sat up looking at him, yawning.

"Myers here."

Cade stood, pulling on his underwear, listening. "Where ya been, Sheriff? Thangs are a brewin'."

Cade rolled his eyes at Sally's informal address over the radio. He had warned her about that a million times.

"Go, Sally, what is it?"

"Tony Somerville's house is ablaze. We can't raise Struthers on his cell or radio. The fire alarms are going off over at the high school."

Damn. It never seemed to end. Cade watched Mary get up and start to fold the linens they used.

Sitting on the sofa, he gave Sally direction. "Make sure the firehouse is sent to where the confirmed fire is. Send Deputy Lockhart to Struthers' house. Have Deputy Boyd meet me at the school and alert the State Troopers they may have to pick up some of our slack. Have one of the troopers come to Mary's place now."

"Ten-four, Sheriff."

Cade signed off and looked at Mary. "Sweetheart, you don't have to get up. It's only three-thirty in the morning. Go back to bed."

"I'm gonna go to the actual bed, and I want to see you off."

Cade smiled. "You do?"

She walked over to him with the pile of linens in her hands. When she was in front of him, she stood on her toes and puckered her lips.

Cade got the message and leaned over and kissed her.

"Mmm, don't get me started, woman." He playfully swatted her bottom.

She gave a yelp and ran for the stairs. Cade grabbed the sleeping bags and ran up the stairs after Mary.

Mary sat on her bed while watching Cade get dressed. He was so handsome in his uniform. She smiled when he winked at her watching him zip his fly.

"I want to see you today. I am not sure what time I'll be free to come back and spend more time with you."

Mary nodded, still watching him. He put his shoes on and grabbed his belt. "You work today?"

"No, not today. I am having lunch with Lana." She thought of how she wanted to help Cade with his caseload. "I thought I'd go to Mandy's house, check it out, see if her go-bag is still there."

Deeply frowning, Cade shook his head. "No. Absolutely not."

His words were an order. Mary bristled, and her eyebrows rose. "Excuse me."

Cade sighed. He knew that tone. He's heard it from his mom when talking to his father. He's heard it in the past when his brother's girlfriends used it. And he's heard it directed at him several times in the past from his girlfriends. He looked at his current girlfriend, wondering how he could step back out of the pit he seemed to have fallen in.

Mary, completely naked, sitting all prim and proper with a straight back that thrust her beautiful breasts out, didn't help. She was literally the naughty librarian come to life.

Cade was distracted by her beauty and mouth that was now in a disapproving frown. His mind drifted, thinking about her full, sexy lips wrapped around his cock. They hadn't gotten around to that last night during all their sex. His dick twitched in his uniform pants. Cade shook his head. He was supposed to be warning her about going anywhere near Mandy's place without him.

"Sweetheart, please, I don't want you going there alone." Cade reasoned.

Her expression didn't improve. "I won't be alone. You just sent for a trooper to watch my every move."

Sighing again, he walked to her, kneeling, he took her hand. "Baby, please, I need peace of mind while I am out there doing my job."

Mary touched his face. She gently caressed the creases in his forehead, smoothing them. She truly didn't want him to worry. But she also wanted to be her own person and make her own decisions. Remembering the attack in her kitchen, she decided to give in this time.

"For me, please?" Cade pressed when she still hadn't answered.

She nodded and leaned over and kissed him. Cade took over the kiss, tasting her deeply, then groaning when he had to stop. "Damn, I wish I could stay with you all day."

Mary laughed and shook her head. "Again? So soon?" She subconsciously put a protective hand down over her vagina.

Cade frowned. "Mary, did I hurt you?"

She looked away. He used a finger on her chin to bring her gaze back to his. "Truth, Mary."

She answered with a smile. "Cade, I am a little sore. It's been at *least* over a year for me. Only God knows how long it has been before that."

Cade gently kissed her lips, then whispered. "I am sorry that I hurt you. I'll take it easy next time."

Mary laughed and slapped his shoulder. "Don't you dare."

Cade stood, laughing. He finished getting dressed.

Mary put on a robe and went downstairs and made coffee.

Cade was finishing his cup when the trooper arrived. Mary walked him to the door. He turned and looked down at her. "I want to come back, but I really have no idea what time it will be."

Mary went to the little table near the door; reaching in a bowl that held her keys, she took a key out and returned to Cade. She put the key in the front pocket on his uniform shirt. Standing on her tippy toes, she kissed him.

"If it's late, let yourself in and come to bed." She smiled sweetly.

Cade kissed her quickly, tapping her nose. Opening the door, he gave one last direction, "Lock it."

Mary watched him exchange some words with the trooper before getting in his car and heading out with lights flashing.

∞∞∞

Cade met Deputy Boyd in front of the high school. It was still dark outside. Boyd had stopped the firemen from entering as the firemen were off to the side waiting. Like before, there were no outward signs of a fire. He ignored Madson glaring at him, thinking Mendelson must be at the active fire at Somerville's place.

Cade walked up to Boyd, nodding his readiness to proceed. They entered the school via the front, wide double doors, with guns drawn and flashlights out. Cade took the right and Boyd the left. Cade was on high alert as he went through the first door, moving his flashlight in a steady, controlled sweep. He ensured the room was empty, turning the lights on before moving on to the next room.

When Cade got to the office where they had found the murdered John Doe, he wasn't surprised to see the damage. There was a large red X on the door. Red paint-covered nearly every free surface. Cade ensured there was no one in the office and continued on.

It took them over forty minutes to sweep the whole school. It wasn't a big school. The main office, the pool, the lunchroom, and the office where the dead guy was found were the only rooms damaged. Cade realized they were rooms needed daily.

Well, it was a done deal; there'd be no school for the high school kids today.

∞∞∞∞

Kallie groggily reached for her buzzing phone. At the same time, the landline rang. Sitting up, she looked at her phone. One of her parents would get the landline. Looking at her notifications, she rolled her eyes and sighed, not quite decided on answering Casey's calls or texts. He was doing both.

When her notifications' alert continued to buzz. She chose to answer his call rather than his text. Whispering, she said, "What do you want now? I've already committed major crimes for you?"

"I just got the robocall that school is closed today," Casey said with far too much glee than Kallie was comfortable with.

Feeling a headache coming on, Kallie put a hand to her temple. "Seriously, Casey. No more. I don't want to do anything else."

Casey laughed. "Come on, you know you're having fun. And you're happy to have the day off of school."

"O-m-g! You did all of this just to get the day off of school?"

"Kallie, it was fun."

Before she could answer, there was a soft knock on her door. Kallie quickly put the phone under her pillow and feign sleep as her mother opened the door.

"Kallie, sweetie?" Her mother whispered, approaching the bed.

Kallie did a credible job of a yawn and stretch. Mumbling her voice to match someone who had just awaken, "Hey, mom, what is it?"

"The school district called to say there is no school today for you high schoolers."

To distract her mom from the vibration she could feel through her pillow, Kallie joked, "So, you woke me up to tell me I don't have to wake up?"

Her mother laughed, walking to the door. "Sleep in as long as you like."

As soon as her mother closed the door, Kallie snatched her phone from under the pillow. Answering the persistent buzzing, Kallie put the phone to her ear. "Casey, I mean it.

I'm done. If you try to bring me in on any more of your pranks, I'll go straight to Sheriff Myers and tell him *everything*!"

Kallie expected an argument. What she got was complete silence. She knew the line was still engaged. She could hear Casey breathing. Did she make an impact? Was she now boyfriendless again?

During the silence, it occurred to her that although her mom answered the robocall from the school district, Casey had been the one to answer his own robocall.

"Casey, where is Billy?"

He mumbled, "A fire."

He sounded sad to Kallie. Was he doing all this to get his big brother's attention? She felt for Casey and his situation. Casey and Billy's parents had been killed in an accident two years ago. Billy had taken full responsibility for his younger brother. They had moved to Eldred because of a special firemen's training program that Billy had been a part of to get the job as the new recruit at the station when his training was done.

Belatedly, it occurred to Kallie that Casey was alone a lot. Billy was often at work. His shifts were twelve hours long, longer if there was a fire. Kallie's heart ached for Casey. She liked him a lot. He was a loner at school but a cute one. She had spotted him on his first day in Eldred High and had been crushing on him ever since. She had been over the moon when he started to pay attention to her.

"A-are you still my girlfriend?" Casey's sad voice came through the phone loud and clear.

Kallie paused. She liked Casey and wanted to be his girlfriend. But she wanted to do usual teen stuff with him, not clandestine adventures in the middle of the night.

"Yes. I am." She answered with her heart.

She heard his relief via a long exhale.

"But Casey, you have to promise, no more Red x stuff or lawbreaking."

Another silence on the other end. This one much shorter. "I promise. No more around you. Promise Kallie."

As they moved on to the topic of what they would do with their day off, Kallie wondered if she should be worried about Casey's qualifying words 'no more around you.' Did that mean he was going to be doing something when she wasn't around?

Sighing, she decided to take Casey at his word and enjoy just being his girlfriend instead of his partner in crime.

∞∞∞∞

"So what is the hottie trooper doing outside? Where's your hottie sheriff?"

Mary closed the door behind Lana. "Cade had to go to an emergency in the wee hours. He hasn't let me be alone since the attack in my kitchen."

"Well, you weren't alone when that attack happened, if I remember correctly." Lana reminded as she walked to the kitchen where Mary was putting the finishing touches on their lunch.

Following Lana, Mary said, "True. But now, Cade ensures my place is locked up tight, and he doesn't leave until someone is here to replace him."

A teasing smile suddenly graced Lana's face. "Sooo, our cute, hot bod, sheriff, spent the *whole* night?"

Mary shook her head, laughing at Lana's silliness as she took the lemonade out of the fridge.

Mary was walking to the island to set the pitcher of lemonade down when Lana jumped up, laughing and pointing. "Oh my God! You guys really did the deed."

Frowning, Mary placed the pitcher down and quirked a brow. "What are you talking about?"

Lana shook her head and said, "Walk to the sink."

Still confused, Mary turned and walked to the sink, turning back to Lana, "What?"

"You're limping!" Lana accused.

"I am not." Mary countered.

"Okay, not outright limping, but you're walking funny. And I didn't think anything of it, but you're putting your hand protectively towards your lower abdomen."

Mary's eyes widen. She hadn't even realized she was walking with particular care or aware that she moved her hand subconsciously every time she felt a twitch of residual pain. She had downplayed her soreness with

Cade. Her nether regions ached. In a good way, as far as she was concerned, but she had definitely used muscles she hadn't in a very long time or maybe even not at all. *"You got Cade and me having sex from my walk?"*

"Tell me I'm lying." Lana dared.

"You're lying." Mary deadpanned.

Lana laughed and started to choke.

"Serves you right." Mary shook her head, walking back to the island, pouring a glass of lemonade, and passing it to Lana.

Mary gingerly sat on one of the stools in front of one of the place settings she had laid out. There were deli meats and cheeses, several different pieces of bread, crackers, and condiments set in front of them.

"When you're done choking, have a seat and enjoy your lunch." Mary shook her head again as Lana cleared her throat after downing the drink.

Lana took her seat and started preparing a sandwich. "So, seriously, I am right? You guys did the damn thing?"

Mary rolled her eyes and begrudgingly admitted it by nodding.

Lana swallowed a bite of the sandwich and pointed an accusing finger at Mary, talking with a full mouth. "I knew it." She went to the cupboard and grabbed chips, and sat back down. "Okay, dish. Was Mr. Hot Body good in bed?"

"Lana! Really, that's private." Mary blushed.

"Girl, not when it's between us girls. Come on, give."

Mary saw her friend's eager expression and gave in. "Okay. It was great. He's great."

Lana's eyes twinkled. "Even though he fucked you bow-legged? He tore that pussy up!" She hopped up and imitated a drunk, bow-legged cowboy or something while holding her vagina.

"Hey, don't cuss." Mary shook her head at Lana's antics. "Will you sit down and eat."

Lana took her seat and bit her sandwich. After swallowing and taking a swig of her second drink, she said, "All kidding aside, I am happy for you guys. Watching Cade be all lonely and seeing you first physically hurt and emotionally sad really hurt my heart. I felt for you guys. It's awesome you're together."

"Well, I don't know if we're officially together. Neither of us asked the other. Although he did say, I was his woman."

"Guys say shit like that when they're getting hot sex. Hmm, did he ask you for a date again?"

"Not so much a date, but he said he wanted to come back and spend time with me. It could be just sex he wants."

Lana was shaking her head before Mary finished speaking. "Oh, hell, no. That man has been getting hit on from the little, teeny boppers to the little grannies. He's not hurting for a date. He also dated Ally Martin for a while. The man could get sex if he wanted it."

"Ally Martin? The nurse Ally Martin? That Ally Martin?" Mary squeaked out in surprise.

"Uh, yes, that one. What's with the Tweety impersonation?" Lana narrowed her eyes.

"It's nothing. It's just Cade told me he hadn't...."

When Mary trailed off, Lana waved her hand in a circular motion. "Come on, out with it. Cade told you...what?"

"It's just that last night while we were... you know?"

Lana gave another hasty wave, "Yeah, yeah?"

"He said it had been a while for him." Mary's tone was disappointed.

"Girl, please, just because he dated Ally doesn't mean he slept with her."

Thinking back to last night, Mary couldn't really see someone as sexual as Cade going a year without sex.

"I guess."

"Get that fucking look off your face right now. Guys, I mean, decent guys don't go around humping everything that moves. If Cade said it's been a while for him, then it's the truth."

"You're right. He's been nothing but decent and a gentleman with me this entire past year."

Lana's mischievous look was back. "He was good, though, wasn't he?"

Mary couldn't stop the grin from spreading on her face. And when Lana started laughing out loud, she had to join in. "Oh, my, Lana, it was amazing. He made me, uh, um, squirt."

Lana's laughter returned. She hopped up and started dancing, singing. *"Bring a bucket and a mop...extra large and extra hard!"*

"Oh, my God! Would you please sit down!" Mary tried to look serious, but she couldn't while watching Lana attempt to copy some of the moves from the famous video.

Suddenly, Lana grabbed her thigh. "Uh, oh, cramp. I've never been that limber." She joked as she sat.

"You're silly."

"You love it." Lana cracked back.

Mary grew somber. She looked directly into Lana's eyes. "I do, ya know?" Shaking her head, she continued. "If you hadn't been my friend all those months ago, I don't know if I could have survived this condition. You, Mandy and Cade, saved my life. I'll never forget it."

Lana's countenance was a rare sober, and her tone subdued. "Hey, don't get all gooey on me. Mandy and I have been friends since the first day she started work at the elementary school. And you have been my friend from the moment I saw you leave that hospital and you dropped your bag, and I picked it up. We'll always be friends. You're my kind of person, Mary. Good people."

"Likewise." Mary got up and hugged Lana.

Lana cleared her throat as Mary sat back down. "Speaking of our missing Musketeer, have you heard from Mandy? All I get is voicemail."

"Me too."

"We should go check out her place."

Mary paused. "Uh, I promised Cade I wouldn't go there alone without him."

Lana narrowed her eyes speculatively. "Did you promise not to go without him or promise not to go alone?"

Mary's head tilted upward as she recalled her conversation with Cade. "Wellllll, now that you mention it...."

Chapter 10

Cade walked over to Ted Mendelson, leaning against the fire chief's vehicle. "Hey, Ted. What happened here?"

Ted looked over his shoulder at Cade. "It's early yet. The smoke hasn't cleared, literally." He indicated his men raking through the ash, putting out embers. "But there are signs of arson."

"Was Somerville inside?"

"Yes, but he didn't get hurt in the fire."

"You guys got him out in enough time?"

"In time to avoid the worse of the fire, yes, to avoid being hurt, no. If I am not mistaken, those were bullet holes in Mr. Somerville I observed before the ambulance took him away."

"What?" Cade was shocked.

"Yeah, and there are obvious signs that the place was ransacked. Perhaps, Somerville interrupted the intruder. We were able to save most of the building. All the damage is in Mr. Somerville's home office."

Cade nodded, putting a hand up, hailing a trooper that was writing something down. "Thanks, Ted. Can I have a preliminary ASAP?"

"You know I will have it on your desk after I wrap things up here. Matt reported the false alarm at the school."

"Yeah, I just came from there. Nothing but vandalism from the Red X Prankster."

"Damn, that guy is getting on my nerve. The principal and the power outage were dangerous, serious. All this other stuff is just plain annoying."

"Tell me about." Cade tapped the brim of his hat at Ted before walking over to the trooper and offering his hand.

The trooper shook hands with Cade. "Hi, Sheriff Myers. I'm Trooper Ryan Daniels from Troop F."

"Hi, can you tell me anything?"

"Yes. Mr. Somerville was conscious when they pulled him out of the fire. He said he came downstairs after a sound or something woke him. An intruder was searching his home office. Mr. Somerville struggled with the man and then was shot. He said he regained consciousness as a fireman stood over him, calling his name. Mr. Somerville passed out again just before the ambulance took him away. The firemen on scene agree there are signs of arson. The fire inspector is en route. The perp obviously started the fire. Why? Your guess is as good as mine."

Cade nodded, tapping the brim of his hat as the trooper answered a call on his radio.

Walking back to his vehicle, Cade's mind began to swirl with all the information. Damn, things just weren't making sense to him. Getting in his car and starting the engine, he shook his head at all of the police matters instead of focusing on his night with Mary. He sighed, backing out of the driveway, thinking at least Mary's safe.

∞ ∞ ∞

Mary hung up with Dr. Murrow's office as Lana turned into Mandy Odessa's driveway of her small home. It was a lovely home. Built on a little less than an acre of land, it was the surrounding land, trees, and bushes that made Mandy's home truly wondrous to look at. With Mandy's green thumb, she created a lush, green mini paradise.

"Now that you made the appointment with Doc Murrow, you can stop hyperventilating over what Cade will think." Lana parked and looked over at Mary with a satisfied smirk.

Mary felt a little guilty, glancing behind her out the back windshield, ensuring the trooper pulled into the drive right after them. Although Cade hadn't specifically said don't go to Mandy's without *him*, Mary knew that is what he meant by don't go alone. She was feeling guilty, but she was worried about her friend. Mandy, Lana, and she never went more than a day or two without speaking to each other. Several days with Mandy not speaking to her or Lana was unusual.

"Dr. Murrow said he'd fit me into his night schedule. I am seeing him at seven."

"Good, now let's go see what our friend has been up to." Lana got out of the car.

As Mary alighted from the vehicle, the trooper stopped them. "Ladies, please wait while I go check out the surrounding area."

Lana sighed, and Mary nodded. The trooper went to the front door to make sure it was locked. He disappeared around the side of the house.

"This is ridiculous. It's annoying too. What is deputy do-right's name again?"

"His name is Trooper Phil Canton. Don't be annoyed, Lana. I am grateful for his help. I don't feel quite as safe with him as I do when Cade is around, but I am extremely grateful."

"I know. I just don't get why they should shadow you during the day. It's not like you're alone right now. I am with you."

Mary nodded and then reminded Lana, "If memory serves, you were with me last time too. Remember how that turned out?"

"Ouch!" Lana said, shocked, eyes popping wide, and she raised her fingers, making a scratching motion. "And the claws come out, meow."

"Now, come on, you know I didn't mean it that way. I just feel better with the trooper around."

"Okay." Lana sighed.

Trooper Canton returned from behind the house. He gave a nod. "It's all clear. I'll be right outside. Shout if you need me."

"Thank you, Trooper Canton." Mary smiled at him. She turned to Lana. "Now, doesn't that make you feel better?"

Lana rolled her eyes and walked to where Mandy kept her hide-a-key.

∞∞∞

"Sheriff Myers, it doesn't look good," Lockhart said, entering Cade's office.

Cade looked up from reports on his desk from the state lab regarding the library incident. As he expected. The forensics yielded nothing concrete.

"To what are you referring, Deputy Lockhart?"

"We located Larry's car."

"Just his car?"

"Yes, sir. It was abandoned on Route 52 near the red barn that used to be an information center."

"When was the last time you saw Deputy Struthers?"

"Late last night. He wasn't due to work today."

"So what was he doing in a sheriff's car? He doesn't normally take a unit home like you do. He uses his personal car on his off days."

"I know. But he has been talking about Miss Odessa being missing. He said he wanted to check something out. I thought he was talking about doing it when he was back on shift."

"Let's get a BOLO out on Deputy Larry Struthers. Take another, closer, look at his apartment. See if there is anything there to give us a clue as to where he may have gone."

"Yes, sir." Deputy Lockhart turned to leave; Cade called him back.

"Shane?"

"Yes, Sheriff?"

"Be careful."

Deputy Shane Lockhart smiled. "Always am, Sheriff."

Sally Fone walked into Cade's office, passing Shane in the doorway. "Hey Sheriff, that uptown D.A. from N.Y. has called you twice more. I thought you were going to get back to her."

Cade moved files to the side, looking for the preliminary report from the fire inspector that Sally had placed on his desk moments ago.

"Yeah, I'll call. I know what she wants. She's gonna remind me about the Devron case in which I have to testify at the end of the year. She wants to prep me. I don't need prepping."

"Well, her assistant called the first couple of times. This time it was the lady herself." Sally mimicked someone drinking tea with their pinky in the air. "Lady practically accused me of not delivering her message to you."

"I'm sure D.A. Reilly didn't mean it that way. She's probably busy. The city pace is super speed compared to Eldred. I'll make sure to touch base with her later."

"Thank you kindly. Next time, I am giving her your cell number."

Cade shook his head at Sally as she left. He wanted to look at the preliminary report from the fire inspector before joining the search for Deputy Struthers. He also wanted to take a closer look at Somerville's home after the fire inspector cleared it. Things were heating up around Eldred. Cade wasn't just thinking of the recent fire. Once again, he took a moment to think of Mary and smile. Things could be better in town, but they were perfect in his private life.

∞∞∞∞

Mary and Lana walked through Mandy's house, checking for any signs that she had been there in the past few days.

"The cops never found her car?" Lana asked as she closed a drawer in Mandy's kitchen counter.

"No," Mary answered from her spot in front of Mandy's message board on the fridge.

"Well, I'd sure like to know how it was driven away without these." Lana turned to Mary holding Mandy's distinctive bundle of keys.

Mary's eyes widened as she walked to Lana and took the keys from her. "Oh, no, this is not good. She doesn't have a second set. Remember when she had to call a locksmith?"

Lana nodded. "Didn't the cops think it strange that her car is gone, but the keys are still here?"

"Police don't know they're here. They didn't have probable cause to come inside Mandy's house. Technically, no one has officially reported her missing. Cade never said why he was looking for Mandy."

"Should we report her missing?"

"No, the police are already looking for her. And so are we." Mary pocketed Mandy's keys and went to her bedroom. She looked in Mandy's closet where she kept her go-bag. It was missing. "Her go bag is gone."

"You mean that extravagant camping bag she's always adding stuff to?" Lana looked around Mary to the empty spot in the closet where the bag usually sat.

"Yes. It's more than a camping bag. It's for emergencies. She keeps a second set of ID in it and cash."

"This from the woman who doesn't have a second set of keys to her car." Lana joked.

Surprised, Mary looked at Lana.

"What?" Lana paused, inquiring about Mary's look.

"You're right. Mandy's a prepper. She wouldn't forget something as simple as an extra set of car keys. She must have another way to enter her car."

"Why didn't she use it that time she locked her keys inside the car instead of calling a locksmith?"

Mary shook her head, leaving the bedroom. "I don't know. But I am suddenly very interested in the hiking trails Mandy's always trying to get us to go on."

"The ones where the entrance is by that red barn out on fifty-two?"

"That's the one."

"Are we going?" Lana asked with a huge smile.

"Yes, we are?"

∞∞∞∞

CRASH!

"What the heck, Kal?" Casey looked at Kallie's face, gone completely white.

Trembling, Kallie knelt and helped Casey pick up the items she had knocked over and dropped from her hands. The display of beer in glass bottles formed in the shape of a pyramid was now scattered. Some were broken all over the store's floor from Kallie walking into the display. She had also dropped the snack items she and Casey had picked out.

One of the mini-mart's employees hurried over. "Hey, it's okay. I'll get someone to clean up."

Casey stood and took Kallie's hand. He looked at her worriedly. Her hand felt like ice, and she was shaking. He led her outside and around the corner where he had parked his brother's car.

"Hey, hey. What's wrong? You look sick." Casey watched a little color return to her pale cheeks.

"It's him!" Kallie said in a loud whisper. Not that anyone could hear them. They were the only ones parked on this side of the building.

Casey looked around. "Him who? What are you talking about?"

"The guy that killed that black guy at the school. He's in the store right now!" Kallie's voice was much louder but just as scared sounding.

Casey said, "Wait here." Before disappearing around the corner.

Kallie nervously waited. It seemed like forever before Casey reappeared with a grim expression. He went straight to the driver's door and unlocked the doors. "Get in. You're right. It's definitely him."

Kallie quickly got in, buckling her seatbelt. "Where are we going?"

Casey turned in his seat to back out of the parking space. "Far from here."

∞ ∞ ∞

Cade looked through Deputy Struthers' police vehicle. There was nothing to indicate where he was or what happened to him.

"Sheriff, I went back over to his place. No sign of him there either." Deputy Lockhart said.

"I didn't really expect for him to be there. I just wanted to double-check."

"What do you supposed happened?"

Cade shook his head, wondering the same thing. "I honestly don't know." However, he was leaning towards Miss Odessa's disappearance, and Deputy Struthers' disappearance were connected. They were too similar not to be. Plus, the last task Struthers was performing had something to do with Mandy Odessa. The two were definitely connected somehow. But damn if he knew how.

He closed the door and locked it, pocketing the keys. He turned and walked back inside the station as Deputy Lockhart followed.

Earlier, he had formally requested to have five troopers temporarily assigned to Eldred's sheriff station. He had made the request to bolster the sheriff's presence in the community. Looks like they were going to also double as investigators.

∞∞∞∞

"Ms. Smith, I think we should let Sheriff Myers know about this plan of yours." Trooper Canton was looking at Mary and Lana as though they were not too bright.

"Hey, pal, she's a grown-ass woman. She doesn't need permission to go somewhere. And it's none of your business anyway."

Trooper Canton sent a glare Lana's way before returning his gaze to Mary. He implored. "Let me just notify the Sheriff. After all, he asked me to keep him apprised of your movements."

Mary had been willing to compromise with the trooper until he mentioned Cade keeping tabs on her. Cade asking the trooper to basically babysit her made Mary bristle with defiance. As Lana had stated, she was a grown woman. She'll do what she wanted.

"Trooper Canton, I am going up this trail. You can come with me or not." With those strong words of defiance, Mary turned with Lana and went to the trailhead of Mandy's favorite hiking spot.

Mary didn't look back to see if Trooper Canton followed until they were well and truly on the trail. Glancing over her shoulder, she saw him trailing them by a couple of yards. Mary noted that he was speaking into the radio attached to his shoulder.

"I think I should have changed shoes like you." Lana's words brought Mary's attention from the trooper.

"I told you that it would be hard in flats. Mandy is a seasoned hiker and camper. Her favorite trail wasn't going to be a walk in the park."

Lana smirked at Mary's hiking boots she had insisted on changing into before they left to check out Mandy's favorite trail. She was cursing her nonchalant decline of Mary's second pair of hiking boots that were offered.

"Ya know, nobody likes an 'I-told-you-so' smartass." Lana puffed out, almost slipping on moss on a rock.

Mary's hand quickly shot out to lend aid to her friend. "Careful. It's damp and slippery around here. We must be near some type of body of water or something."

"Now, you're Miss Nature?" Lana gibed.

"No. I just know elementary grade science." Mary stuck out her tongue at Lana, laughing when Lana flipped her the bird.

Mary looked back at Trooper Canton. He was talking a mile a minute into his cell. Mary supposed it was better than the radio on his shoulder.

She had decided not to be bothered by Cade's reaction, repeating Lana's take on the situation. She's a grown-ass woman. Besides, she was increasingly scared for Mandy's safety.

Chapter 11

Cade did an about-face, almost crashing into Deputy Lockhart. He was listening to Trooper Canton on his cell phone. He wasn't paying attention to his surroundings since he answered the call.

"Sheriff, I need you to take this call on line two. It's that annoying D.A. And there is someone from the Marshal's Service on line one. They say it's very important." Sally shouted at Cade's retreating back.

Lockhart stepped aside and turn to follow the Sheriff. "What's going on?"

Cade put a hand over the cellphone and said, "Get in your car and go to the red barn on fifty-two. Code three." Lockhart nodded and ran to his parked unit in the front of the building.

Cade made his way to his car, continuing to speak with Trooper Canton. "Why didn't you stop her? You're there to protect her, even from herself."

"With all due respect, sir, Miss Smith has a mind of her own. She was insistent. The other one egged her on."

Canton's words came through the phone crystal clear, especially the ones he didn't actually speak. He hinted that Mary was a handful and Lana wasn't helping matters with her personality, which could seem, at times, extremely abrasive and cavalier.

"Okay. I am on my way. Try to slow them down. They already have a big head start." Cade didn't wait for a response. He put his phone on his belt and got in his car. He needed to decrease the women's head start. He put on his lights and siren and went speeding after Lockhart.

∞∞∞∞

Mary didn't know how she was doing it or why she was able to do it. But she was seeing definite signs of someone using the trail recently. Sudden mental images flooded her head. She could identify the trees, the vegetation, the harmless and the harmful. She knew she was heading West without knowing why she was so positive about her direction. Instinctively she knew the signs she saw would not have been there to see or track if they were older than a few days.

Mary paused at the word track. That's precisely what she was doing. She was tracking someone in the woods, reasonably deep woods with a moderate trail. *Wait! How did she know that?* Mary nodded to herself as she picked up other telltale signs that the trail was moderate instead of beginner or advanced. The trail was just a bit too much for beginners and not enough, far too easy for someone of advanced level.

Mary's footsteps increased as she saw sign after sign of someone making a mad dash through some of the bushes. Her confidence rose, and she picked up even more speed when more visible signs showed something had happened in the woods.

Following her leads, Mary went off the trail, entering the denser and less used section of the trail.

"Hey, wait!" Lana panted out.

Mary hadn't realized the gap between her, Lana, and Trooper Canton had steadily increased. Ignoring Lana, choosing to not stop, Mary continued on, following her instincts. Her instincts told her that something happened on the trail and continued into the much thicker, unruly bushes.

"Mary, we can't see you anymore. Hey!" Lana called from a distance, still on the clearly marked trail.

"Miss Smith?" Trooper Canton called out.

Mary couldn't stop. She quickened her pace, ducking brambles, working around stumps, thick brush, and stones. Her heart rate hammered in her ears. A new smell assailed her nostrils. *She knew that smell!*

Rushing around a vast bolder, Mary spied another thick bramble, leaves, and bushes. Mary tilted her head to the side. Again, she knew something definite and didn't know how she knew. Unlike the others she traversed so far, there was something unnatural about this particular bramble, weeds, leaves, and branches. Mary began pulling at it. She pulled and pushed obstacles until she uncovered the body.

There was a ringing in her ears. Her face grew flush, nausea attacked her stomach, then everything went black.

∞ ∞ ∞

"We should go to Sheriff Myers!" Kallie was hyperventilating with fear.

"No, are you stupid? If we tell him we can identify the killer, he's gonna figure it out real quick that the reason I saw the killer is because I am the Red X Prankster." Casey shook his head. "Fuck that! I'm not trying to go to jail. Billy would lose his shit!"

"This is more important than your brother being mad at you. That man is dead, and the killer didn't leave. What if he's here to kill someone else?"

Casey chewed the corner of his mouth then shook his head. "Nah, if he was here to kill someone else, he would have done it already."

"You don't know that, Casey."

Casey touched Kallie's hand, gently taking it in his. "Please, Kallie, don't tell. I swear if there was a chance of that guy killing again, I'd go straight to Sheriff Myers myself. Give me some time to tell Billy. Then, we will go to the police together."

Kallie looked into Casey's gorgeous eyes. Sighing heavily, she said, "Okay, but only twenty-four hours. I don't think it's good to not report what we saw."

"Witnessing a crime and not reporting it is not a crime, Kallie."

Shaking her head, she threw Casey a disappointed look. Snatching her hand from his, she countered. "It should be."

∞ ∞ ∞

Cade slammed on the breaks, haphazardly parking next to Lockhart, who was getting out of his car.

"Where are we going?" Shane asked, checking his weapon.

Cade rushed to the red barn that used to be an information center about the hiking trails beyond it. Budget cuts resulted in the city closing the information center down. It was free to hike the trails. People could come by and still get information via booklets and notices posted on a board inside the barn. There were vending machines inside filled with hiker's needs. It was unlocked every morning and locked every night by deputies. The supplies were replenished by an independent vendor.

Pulling the door open, Cade took a quick scan to make sure no one was inside, calling out in case someone was in the bathroom. When there was no answer, he headed towards the trail.

"Let's go. They have a serious head start on us." Cade instructed as he started an evenly paced jog on the trail.

Several moments later, the trail became a steady incline. Cade took a look behind him to see Deputy Lockhart had dropped back several more yards. He couldn't wait for him. He had to make sure Mary was okay. Cade couldn't understand the sense of urgency he felt regarding Mary. She brought all his emotions and feelings forth without even trying. No woman before her had him feeling this way. He needed to get to her.

∞ ∞ ∞

"Mary! Mary! Answer me right now!" Lana screamed.

Trooper Canton ran up to Lana. "Where is she?"

"I don't know. She took off in there somewhere!" Lana yelled, flinging her arm in the general direction Mary took.

Canton forced his way into the thick brush. "Miss Smith!"

He made his way slowly through the thick woods, all the while calling for Mary. He was dripping sweat, even though it wasn't hot out. By the time he came across Mary Smith out cold on the ground next to a dead body, he was soaked in sweat.

Canton swiftly pulled his weapon as he inched closer, reaching out to check Mary's pulse while still looking around. There wasn't anyone in the immediate vicinity. Whatever had happened was done with. He looked at Mary out cold on the ground. She must have fainted.

Holstering his weapon, he took off his jacket, balling it into a pillow shape and putting it under Mary's head. He tried to rouse her. "Mary. Mary, can you hear me?"

Nothing.

Canton became aware of Miss Miles screaming and yelling for both him and Mary.

He shouted out, "It's okay, Miss Miles. I've got her."

While Lana yelled a bunch of questions, Canton called in for the coroner, CSI team, and rolled paramedics.

∞∞∞∞

Cade didn't stop when he heard the calls for assistance over his radio. He picked up speed. He tripled timed his rush up the trail. He thanked God he was physically fit. He had done this trail before several times. But never at this neck-break speed. And never with this much anxiety.

He took a glance behind him to see Deputy Lockhart was back in his line of vision. Cade had been going so fast he had left the deputy behind. Lockhart had picked up the pace considerably to catch back up with Cade.

Several moments later, Cade heard Lana's voice, yelling at someone. Cade pushed his limits, rushing until he had eyes on Lana. He didn't see Trooper Canton or Mary. A stone formed in the pit of his stomach.

He came abreast, Lana. She was so distraught she hadn't realized he was upon her until he touched her. She was startled and screamed the place down.

"Lana! It's me. It's Cade!"

She threw herself at him. Cade held her trembling body, trying to calm her.

"Lana, where is Mary and Trooper Canton?"

She pointed vaguely over her shoulder. He didn't see anything. He was about to shake her and ask again when Trooper Canton called out.

"We're here, Sheriff."

Passing Lana off to Deputy Lockhart as he arrived, Cade followed the trooper's voice.

Fuck! What were they doing off the trail? Cade pushed through until he arrived where Trooper Canton was kneeling.

The scene that met his eyes was a tableau of horror. Mary was sprawled on the ground, completely out. There was a dead body not too far from her. His keen observation allowed him to assess the situation quickly.

The body was older than two days, there were some obvious signs of trauma to its face and arms. The smell was one he'd never forget. Decomp was a smell that stayed with a person.

He rushed to Mary's side. Kneeling, he checked her pulse, and she had no apparent signs of harm.

"Fainted?" He put the question to Canton.

"Yeah, I think so."

His words pissed Cade off. While he repositioned himself on the ground and pulling Mary into his arms, he threw a glare at the trooper. "What do you mean, 'I think so'? Don't you know?"

"Sir, she was very insistent on coming up here. And I am not trying to deflect blame here. I take full responsibility for this situation. But Miss Smith was like a mountain goat or something. She was like an expert rushing up here. She left Miss Miles and me in the dust."

Cade looked down at Mary's angelic face. She had a slight frown between her brows, as though even unconscious, she was bothered.

Cade looked at Trooper Canton. Like himself, he was drenched in sweat. Cade realized his breathing was just returning to normal. He hadn't paid much attention to himself or his discomfort. He only knew he had to get to her to protect her.

Subconsciously, he pulled Mary closer to his chest.

She stirred, mumbling.

Cade put his ear closer to her mouth. His expression turned grimmer as he understood the words she uttered.

"Mike. Mike. Help me, please. Mike."

With a sense of dread and loss, Cade pulled her tighter to him, slightly rocking her.

∞∞∞∞

Mary came to slowly, but she felt warm and safe. There was a low constant humming. She tried opening her eyes, but something was holding them closed. The hum became clearer; someone was talking.

"What the hell were you doing?"

"Hey, pal, don't yell at me. I didn't do a thing."

"Only, egged her on to be reckless. Aren't you her friend? You're supposed to help keep her safe and unharmed!"

"I'm not the one who had her limping all day!"

"Limping? What the fuck are you talking about?"

"Oh, so now you got amnesia. You weren't the one who fucked her so hard she could barely walk?"

"Holy hell. She told you that?"

"No! In fact, she denied it. But I told her she was limping and unknowingly putting a protective hand near her hoo-ha like it was sore, or someone was gonna attack it again."

"Shit! I didn't mean to hurt her."

"Well, according to her, you didn't, and it was fantastic for her. Besides, she didn't feel the pain when we got on the frigging trail."

"What happened? She was supposed to be seeing Dr. Murrow."

"She did arrange to meet him. He gave her an evening appointment tonight at seven."

There was a pause, and then the voices continued.

"You still shouldn't have encouraged her to walk the trail. I know you guys are worried about Mandy. My men will find her."

"Me? Encourage her? Dude, she needed no encouragement from me. Cade, you should have seen her. It was like watching a hound dog or something. Well, until we lost sight of her. Man, can she move when she wants to."

In her mind, Mary pounced on the name. Cade? Yes, please, she wanted Cade. She needed Cade. She moaned.

"Oh, she's coming to."

Mary felt his touch before she heard him. A gentle hand touched her cheek as his voice drew her to full consciousness. "Mary, baby, can you hear me? It's Cade."

She tried to speak. "Cade?" Her voice came out raspy and low.

"Yes, sweetheart. It's me. I've got you. You're safe."

"Cade, there w-was a b-body."

Cade leaned down, touching his cheek to hers, kissing her softly. "Ssh, I know, baby. It's being taken care of. I am worried about you."

Her lashes fluttered, and she opened her eyes all the way. Cade's beautiful blue eyes hooked her complete attention.

"Cade! Thank God!" Mary sounded relieved. "I thought I was dreaming you saving me."

"No, it's not a dream. I am really here." Cade frowned. "Although, you didn't really need saving. You overdid it and passed out when you found the body."

Mary tried sitting up, and the room spun. Putting a hand to her forehead, she moaned. "Ugh, this room is spinning."

"Take it easy." Cade put a gentle hand to her shoulder, guiding her to lie back down.

"Yes, you need rest." Ally Martin said from the door.

Cade stepped back from the bed as Ally came to check the monitors that Mary was hooked up to. Ally looked Mary directly in the eyes. "Truth, how do you feel?"

Mary took a deep breath and took a mental catalogue of her body's aches and pains. "Other than a few aches and pains and a massive headache, I am okay, I think."

"Well, you have a bump to the back of your head. You probably hit it when you fainted."

Mary reached for the back of her head, locating the egg-sized knot immediately. It was where the pain was pounding most.

"The doctor wants to do a cat scan. He's worried about all the knocks to the head you've had lately."

"Ally, are they keeping her?" Cade asked.

"Well, that will be up to the doctor and, of course, Mary herself. But she's definitely going to be here for a couple more hours at least."

Ally made some adjustments to the monitor before telling Mary she'd be back to get her for her test.

"I'll stick around with you until they decide whether or not to keep you." Lana offered.

"Unless I need surgery, I am not staying. I am going home to get some rest." Mary said, looking at Cade.

"I want-"

Before Cade could finish what he was about to say, there was a knock on the door.

Avoiding Cade's disapproving look, Mary answered, "Come in."

It was Deputy Shane Lockhart. "Sorry to bother you, Sheriff. There is an urgent message from the Marshal's Service."

Cade's brow furrowed, "What is it?"

Lockhart indicated that Cade should come closer so the other occupants in the room couldn't hear. Cade moved to the door by Lockhart.

"It appears we have missing federal agents. Their last check-in was from Eldred, NY."

Chapter 12

Cade walked back to Mary's bed, leaning over and giving her a kiss. He held her gaze. "I'll be back. We're gonna have a conversation about you staying if the doctors suggest it."

Mary solemnly nodded before kissing him again.

Cade looked at Lana. "Keep an eye on her."

Lana nodded too, grabbing a chair near the window and bringing it close to the bed. "I'm not going anywhere."

Cade left with Lockhart.

Lana looked closely at Mary.

Mary caught her gaze, started to feel uncomfortable with Lana's scrutiny. She sat up straighter. "What? What's that look for?"

"Girl, whatever happened to you a year ago, it wasn't because you were a defenseless, vulnerable woman," Lana said with suspicion.

"What are you talking about?" Mary didn't like the look Lana was giving her.

"*Mary*, it was like someone flick a switch inside of you. You were not Mary. You were... whoever you used to be."

Mary worried her lip between her teeth. "I don't know where it was coming from, but when I was up on that trail, information just flooded my head."

"Well, you must have been a hound dog in another life." Lana jested.

"The way I feel right now, I'd take it."

Lana relented a little. "I was angry with you, but now I have to thank you for the cardio."

They laughed. Then Lana continued more seriously. "Don't worry, Mary. Cade will find out who you are and what happened to you. It's not only his job, but he also has a vested interest. Don't worry."

Mary wasn't convinced, but she smiled anyway, hoping that Lana's words would be valid.

∞ ∞ ∞

"Sorry for pulling you out of there." Lockhart apologized. "I know you wanted to spend some time with Mary."

"It's okay. What's this about a missing agent from the Marshal's service?"

"Sally said she's been trying to relay their message to you. Here's the number. They want you to call back ASAP."

Cade took the offered piece of paper. "The doctors had to put Somerville in a medically induced coma, so we can't speak to him about his break-in." Feeling the weight of his office, Cade sighed, running a hand across the back of his neck. "Lockhart, I tell you something hinky is going on. There is just too much criminal activity for it all not to be related somehow."

Lockhart shook his head. "What? You mean, like the same person is responsible for all this stuff happening?"

Cade nodded. "Think about it, except for the Red X Prankster and possibly Mary's stalker, all these other things happened about the same time. Mandy Odessa missing, the dead guy at the school, Somerville's break-in, and arson, Deputy Struthers missing, this new dead guy in the woods. All this, in a town that practically had no crime, suddenly it's a hotbed of illegal activity." Cade shook his head. "I don't buy it."

"Okay, if they are connected, there has to be a common denominator for all this activity."

Cade shook his head. "Other than Eldred, I can't see anything."

Lockhart shook his head too. "Maybe some light will be shed by the reports. They should be coming in soon, yeah?"

"Yes, I am headed to the station to return the call to the Marshal's service and look at what the labs have sent over. The state troopers will be backing us up overall, but they are also sending three troopers to be specifically assigned to Eldred's sheriff's station. I need you to stay here until I get back. They should be keeping Miss Smith. Miss Miles is in there with her, and she said she'd stay until it's decided if Miss Smith stays."

Shane Lockhart smiled. "Do you really think Miss Smith will stay?"

Cade didn't smile. "Oh, she'll stay."

Shane laughed as he watched the sheriff walk away, convinced he'd keep Miss Smith in the hospital if she didn't want to be there.

∞∞∞∞

"What are you kids up to today?" Billy Tillman asked his little brother Casey and his new girlfriend, Kallie.

"Nothing, just hanging out. We might go to the mall later."

Billy had already stopped listening. He made agreeable sounds while looking at the piled-up mail for the week. "Uh-huh, okay. Please make sure you're in by curfew."

Casey scowled. "I thought that was just for Halloween."

"Sheriff Myers extended it until further notice. I am working another double, so I won't see you for another twenty-four hours. You kids make sure you're inside by curfew."

"Okay." Casey and Kallie chorused, watching Billy grab his keys and leave.

Kallie waited until she heard Billy's car leave the drive. "He just got back last night. I thought he was going to spend time with you; watch the game you recorded for him?"

Casey gave a credible show of nonchalance. "I guess he forgot and has better things to do." Casey stomped off to his bedroom, leaving Kallie at the kitchen table to follow him or not.

∞∞∞∞

Dr. Dan Murrow assessed Mary Smith's chart. He was aware of the sharp eyes in the room on him. After reading her chart, his eyes sought out the only eyes that mattered to him—his patient's.

"Mary, I see the doctors are concerned by your multiple hits to the head. I have to admit, I am too."

"I am okay. Just a little disoriented at first and some pain." Mary sounded as if she was trying to convince herself rather than Dr. Murrow.

The doctor turned to Lana. "Could you please excuse us, Ms. Miles?"

Lana hopped up, "Sure thing, doc." She turned to Mary, "I'll go grab something to eat and then check back in with you."

Mary nodded. "Thanks for being here."

"No problem." Lana left, leaving the room a bit dull.

"Mary, you must see that we, doctors, are only looking out for your best interests."

"Sure, I can see that. It's just I think I know what I feel physically. I don't think I need to be here overnight."

Dr. Murrow sighed. "Tell me what's been happening with your memory."

Taking a seat and removing a small recorder from a breast pocket, he started the recorder, stating the date, time, and place and identifying himself, and referring to Mary as patient number three-five-nine.

"Okay, when you're ready. Tell me what you've been experiencing regarding your memory."

Mary took a deep breath and began in a low voice that gained strength as she described her feelings. "Well, it's a bit vague sometimes, like viewing a picture or scene through smoke or a waterfall. I can see some things but can't make them out fully."

"How does that make you feel?"

"Frustrated. Very, very frustrated."

"You said 'sometimes' it's vague. Are there other times when your recall is clearer?"

"Yes, and it's not like the images I can't make out. It's more of a feeling coming from somewhere deep down inside me. Like today when I was on that trail. I knew things."

Dr. Murrow encouraged her to elaborate with a nod.

"Up there on that trail, I knew beyond a shadow of a doubt that something happened up there. I saw the clear indications of a struggle. I knew the signs." Mary moved her hands in emphasis. "I mean, I just knew them, like, poof, I knew how to track the incident to my ultimate find, the body."

"And finding the body? How did that make you feel?"

Mary's eyes widen as if it were obvious. "I fainted."

Dr. Murrow sat forward a little in his seat. "Your fainting was a reaction to how you were feeling, not the feeling itself." His eyes penetrated hers. His eyes medically assessing. "How did you *feel*, Mary?"

Mary closed her eyes and brought back the image of her finding the body. "I-I was scared."

"You don't sound convinced, Mary." Dr. Murrow observed. "Were you terrified?"

With her eyes still closed, a furrow appeared on her brow and a frown on her lips. "Yes, I was scared. But..."

Dr. Murrow picked up on her hesitation and prompted. "But what, Mary?"

"I wasn't afraid of the body." She simply said in a small voice.

"What scared you, Mary?"

Her eyes sprang open and sought out the doctors. "I was afraid of the knowledge I had and where it came from. Why did I know the trail was unnaturally disturbed? Why was I able to track the signs? Why did I know that the body was at least three days dead? Why was I not scared while tracking and discovering the body? Why did I have a deep-down satisfaction, looking at the dead body? Why was I so dispassionate about a man dying?"

Mary abruptly stopped talking, realizing her tone was starting to carry the anxiety she felt. Looking worriedly at the doctor, she asked. "So, am I crazy, doc?"

Dr. Murrow gave his habitual pause, collecting his thoughts before speaking. "No, Mary. I don't think you are crazy. However, I think you are going through some form of memory recovery that is vivid and intense. It is taking a physical toll on your body and may be hampering your complete recovery."

"I feel like I am crazy."

"I'll tell you what I'd like to do if you are agreeable."

"Yes?"

"I have had some very successful hypnotizing sessions with patients, not all my patients, mind you. There have been a few who have benefited greatly from a session or two."

Mary's eyebrows climbed to her bangs. "Hypnosis? Seriously?"

Dr. Murrow chuckled. "I hear some skepticism in your voice. True, not everyone can be hypnotized. But it couldn't hurt. It might even help you."

Sighing and stretching a little, Mary said with feeling. "At this point, doc, I am willing to try anything to get back to whatever my normal was."

"If you're feeling up to it, why don't we keep your seven o'clock appointment tonight?"

"Yes, I'd appreciate that. Is it okay if I bring someone with me?"

"I don't see why not. It's your confidentiality to share or not."

"I'd like Sheriff Myers with me. I feel safe with him, nothing against you. I just feel better when he's around. And he asked if he could come."

"No problem. Wear something comfortable, eat too." Dr. Murrow turned off the recorder.

Standing, he came closer to the bed, touching her hand in reassurance; he smiled. "No more stressing, young lady. We'll get you on the road to recovery very soon."

"I hope so. It's been a year."

There was a courtesy knock on the door before it inched open. "Hey, is it safe?" Lana asked.

"Yes, Lana, come in." Mary waved her inside the room.

Lana came inside the room bearing goodies from the hospital cafeteria. "I got some stuff I think you might like, and I definitely do."

"Well, I'll leave you ladies to it." Dr. Murrow said as he pulled the chair closer to the bed for Lana. "I'll see you tonight, Mary."

Dr. Murrow left, and Lana placed her cafeteria haul on Mary's bedside table. "What's happening tonight?"

"My appointment with Dr. Murrow."

"I thought he just had one with you."

"We talked. But he wants to try something to help push my memories to the forefront."

"So, you're just planning on leaving no matter what the doctors say?" Lana was disapproving as she picked up a Jell-O cup, grabbing a spoon, and started eating.

"I mean, if the doctors say I must stay, I will. Dr. Murrow can come back here."

"Okay. That's reasonable." Lana set down the Jell-O she was eating and picked up a chocolate pudding, handing it to Mary. "Here's your favorite, eat something."

Reluctantly, Mary took the offered treat. She wasn't in the mood, and she was pretty sure Ally Martin asked that she not eat anything until after her cat scan. What she really wanted was Cade. She felt unsure and unsteady lately when he wasn't around. She needed his presence to feel whole. Without Cade, her damaged memory plagued her with uncertainty and fear.

She hoped he'd return soon. But knew he was most likely too busy to even make it to her appointment with Dr. Murrow no matter his desire to be there with her.

She was just about to ask Lana to come with her if Cade couldn't make it when there was a knock on the door, and then it opened to reveal the greeting smile of the local heart throb teacher, Stan Horiwitz.

"Hello, Mary. I came to see how you were doing?"

Surprised, Lana stood, facing him, asking, "How did you even know she was here? She isn't even formally admitted yet."

Although he answered Lana's question, his eyes were on Mary. "Oh, I was here visiting Tony Somerville. It's awful what happened. On my way to his ICU room, I saw the ambulance arrive with you."

Mary recalled Cade's suspicions of the jovial-looking English teacher. She felt her anxiety intensify, and she thought, *Oh, help. Where are you, Cade?*

∞∞∞

Cade sat at his desk, listening to the phone ring in his ear while wading through all the paperwork accumulated on his desk in the past several days. He had phone messages, lab reports, arson reports, and routine daily paperwork that hadn't been touched.

"Hello, Special Agent Collin Pierce."

A smile came to Cade's face at the sound of his old buddy's voice. "Hey, Brother. It's good to hear your voice."

"Oh, wow! Cade? Cade Myers! How the hell are you, bro?"

"I'm good, good. And I really want to swap catch-up stories with you, but I called for a favor. I am swamped and drowning here. I need your professional reach where mine ends."

"Swamped? Drowning? I thought you moved to some Podunk town so you wouldn't have to deal with being swamped and drowning? What was it, Elder?"

"Ha, very funny. I see you haven't lost your sense of humor in FedsVille. It's *Eldred*. I need help with something official and personal."

"Uh, oh. Do I want to know what the personal part is?" Collin was cautious.

"It's a woman," Cade said.

"Uh, oh." Collin's caution grew.

"She's a victim." Hearing how that sounded, Cade amended, "Well, she was a victim. Now she's a productive member of society. The problem is she's a complete amnesiac. I found her a little over a year ago on the side of the road, beaten and left for dead. I did all the usual stuff to find out her I-D. Nothing has worked. I exhausted all the databases I have access to. I was wondering if you can go that extra fed-mile and see if we can find out who she is for her and for me."

"Cade, are you involved with this woman?"

"Yes." Cade was succinct.

"Bro, you didn't learn anything from my mistake?"

"Collin, you made a victim your girlfriend, and then she turned on you. You're lucky it turned out okay."

"That's what I mean. This could blow up in your face."

"Mary is so sweet and kind." Cade defended his involvement with Mary.

"Uh, huh. I bet her looks had nothing to do with it?"

"She's humble and caring."

"And?"

"She has a wonderful sense of humor." Cade tried again.

"And?" Collin wasn't buying it.

"All right, you asshole. Mary is stunningly beautiful, in face and body."

Collin's laughter was loud through the phone. Cade held the receiver away from his ear for several seconds.

"Are you done being a jackass?"

"Yeah, I am. For now." Collin sighed. "Listen, I only tell you this as a friend. Be careful."

"I hear you. This woman is amazing."

"I've never heard you talk about a woman like this before. I must also warn that if she's so amazing, she could already be taken."

Cade ignored the warning and the recall of Mary calling out another man's name. "I have everything under control, including my heart."

"Man, I hope so. Okay, give me the details on your Mary."

"I sent you an email with attachments with all the lab reports on her, fingerprints, physical description, and all the databases I tried."

"Okay, I'll check it out, run it through some of the FBI's washers. I'll get back to you as soon as I know something."

"Thanks, Collin. I owe you one."

"You owe me nothing. I can't count the times you were there for me. Consider it repayment."

"This is a little above and beyond."

"Not for someone I consider family. Talk to you soon. Take care, bro." Collin disconnected.

Cade kept the receiver in his hand, pressing the hang-up and releasing it quickly. He dialed the number to the Marshal Service on the paper Lockhart had given him.

"Morrison?" The phone was answered abruptly.

"Hello, this is Sheriff Cade Myers in Eldred, NY returning Agent Flynn Morrison's call."

"Sheriff Myers! Thank God! I'm Flynn."

The agent's distress came clearly through the line. "How can I help you?"

"Two of my agents were dispatched to your town to retrieve a witness we had placed there. You know her as Mandy Odessa."

"Yes, I met Marshal Zack Duncan. I took him to a couple of locations where Mandy could possibly be, or someone there possibly knew where she was or was headed. The leads didn't pan out. Your Marshal said he'd stick around see if he could pick up her trail."

"You say Marshal Duncan was alone?"

"He was when I met him and when I saw him later in the day."

"Marshal Duncan was with Marshal Aster Winter."

"No, Marshal Duncan was definitely alone."

There was silence for several seconds on the Marshal's end. Then he said, "I am coming to you. I haven't been able to hail either of my men. And there is evidence that the hitman, Never-Miss, is headed to Eldred for a critical witness. The Dulca crime family has tried twice before to get Mandy and Eldred was her third location. We figure the infamous Never-Miss is their last resort. My people are top-notch agents, and they wouldn't go silent or missing without the situation being dire."

Worried for the Marshals, Cade offered. "I'll head over to the hotel where Marshal Duncan was staying and see if there are any clues as to where your Marshals are headed."

"Thank you, Sheriff Myers. I appreciate your help. I'll see you soon. I'm just reentering the country."

"See you soon, Marshal." Cade hung up deep in thought.

Cade stood to leave to go check the hotel. Worry etched his face. He had a suspicion that the infamous hitman wasn't headed to Eldred but had already arrived. Never-Miss is why everyone was missing; Mandy, the Marshals, and Cade didn't know how, but he believed the hitman was also responsible for Struthers' absence.

Chapter 13

Cade swiped the key card the lady at the reception desk gave him for Marshal Duncan's room. Immediately upon entering, Cade knew it was empty. The room had signs of a struggle. There was overturned furniture, the mattress on the bed was askew, and there was a fist-size hole in the wall. The bathroom sink had blood smears and droplets along the rim.

Cade checked the drawers finding exactly what he expected, nothing. Marshal Duncan's clothes were still in the suitcase on the rack in the corner of the room. His weapon and ID were missing. Cade hoped it was the Marshal who was the victor of the fight that had gone on.

He found no signs of anyone other than one person staying in the hotel room. The receptionist said Marshal Duncan had checked in alone, and she didn't know when he left. There were absolutely no signs of the other agent.

Cade did another once over of the room before calling in the state CSI team. He'd have to call Agent Flynn Morrison and given him the disappointing update.

∞∞∞∞

"Well, I think you should have stayed," Lana said as she followed Mary through her front door.

"I am fine. Just a little sore."

Lana smirked. "You were sore to begin with, before we even left the house."

Mary turned and gave Lana a smirk of her own. "Not that kind of sore. I am sore from the trail, and I admit my head hurts a tiny bit from hitting the ground when I fainted."

"Uh-huh, just a tiny bit?" Lana shook her head, going to Mary's kitchen and raising her voice. "Go get comfortable on the sofa. I'll bring you aspirin for your head. It was crazy to turn down prescription-strength painkillers at the hospital."

Raising her voice to be heard in the kitchen, Mary sat on the sofa, using the throw blanket on the back of the sofa to cover herself. "I don't like that loopy feeling I get. Besides, I want to be clear-headed when I have my appointment with Dr. Murrow."

"I guess," Lana answered from the kitchen.

"Speaking of my appointment, can you come with, if Cade can't make it?"

"I'll do you one better. I'll come with whether Cade makes it or not."

"Okay, great."

Lana came in with a tray. On it was water, aspirin, a cup of tea, and some ginger cookies. "This should make you feel better."

"Thanks for doing this and sticking with me."

"I have to admit, I am a bit scared you're gonna end up missing like Mandy. Then I'd have no friends. I can't believe both of you were in trouble, and I didn't even know it."

"You're a great friend. You knew all there was to know about us. If Mandy is in trouble, the only reason she didn't tell us would be because she didn't know she was in trouble until it was too late."

Sitting down, Lana watched Mary take the aspirin with some water and slowly sip her tea. "I hope you're right."

Mary nodded, showing Lana confidence that was all for show. She, too, was very worried about Mandy.

∞ ∞ ∞

Cade was back at the station going over reports he had only a chance to glance at before. Most of the reports revealed very little or what was expected. What wasn't expected was the DNA and prints from the dead guy at the school received a red flag: *Restricted Classified*.

What the hell? Cade snatched up his phone and dialed the state lab. He asked for the tech that signed off on the reports.

"Dillon McConelly, here." A deep baritone greeted Cade after he was transferred three times.

"Hello, Dillon. I am hoping you can help me. I had a homicide here in Eldred that your lab did the forensics and trace for. I received reports back, but the DNA and fingerprint reports all read classified. Can you help me?"

"When we get results like that, it usually means that the information in part or in whole is classified, an 'eyes only' type of deal. You have to have a classification rank to even view the results. It's above my pay grade."

"Can you direct me to whom I should speak to about getting a full report?"

"No, again, it's above my pay grade. I suspect you'll be hearing from them very soon. The person who put the flag on the reports was notified the same time you were. I suggest you hang tight."

"Okay, thank you." Cade hung up, wondering who and what kind of trouble had wandered into his small town.

∞∞∞

"Pardon me, Miss Smith, I think we should wait for the Sheriff." Shane Lockhart was starting to sympathize with Trooper Canton. His eyes switched between the two ladies giving him a look that screamed, 'You're such a guy.'

"I have an appointment with Dr. Murrow. I don't want to be late." Mary explained.

"Don't get your panties in a bunch. Cade can meet us there." Lana said, walking down the front porch steps.

Shane rolled his eyes and followed the ladies to Mary's car. "Miss Smith, everything all locked up?"

Mary smiled at Shane. "Ye—"

"Sheesh, dude, we get it. You're protecting her. Chill."

Shane tried to keep his temper in check, but Miss Smith's friend was ticking him off. "Just doing my job, Miss Miles." Shane's tone dripped politeness he was not feeling.

Looking sheepish, Mary apologized for Lana. "Sorry, Deputy Lockhart. I promise, I feed her and give her water."

And just like that, Shane's good mood was restored. He laughed and opened Mary's door. He ignored Lana, flipping him the bird before getting in the passenger seat.

Shane got in his vehicle and followed them out of the driveway.

∞∞∞

Kallie stood across the street from the sheriff's station. Even close to her destination, she still hadn't decided on what she was going to say. Casey was her new boyfriend, and she wanted to be loyal to him. On the other hand, she was aware of the seriousness of the situation and her responsibility as a member of society.

Squaring her shoulders, she started across the street. Before she got two paces, she froze. As though her thoughts caused his manifestation, the subject of her thoughts was getting in a car in front of a building across the street. It was two spots down from the sheriff's station. Kallie quickly turned back. In the shelter of the city hall's awning, she watched the man who had killed the black man in her school backing out of his parking spot and heading out of town.

∞∞∞

Trooper Canton stood in Cade's office with two of his fellow troopers, Daniels and Decker. Deputy Boyd stood with them.

"Hey, Sheriff Myers, we are assigned to Eldred's station until further notice. These are Troopers Ryan Daniels and David Decker."

Cade took the papers from Trooper Canton. "Welcome aboard, fellas." Cade stood and shook the men's hands. "We sure appreciate the help. You guys will be taking up the slack in our patrolling."

Sally came to the doorway. "Sheriff, you told me to remind you of your appointment with Mary. And Kallie Kramer is here to see you."

Cade looked at Kallie, standing nervously in his doorway with Sally. "Hey, sweetheart, what can I do for you?"

"Can I talk to you, Sheriff Myers?"

Just then, Cade's radio crackled to life. "Sheriff Myers, Lockhart here, come in."

Holding a finger up to Kallie, Cade directed, "Guys, please go with Deputy Boyd. He can give you your patrol assignments."

The troopers, Boyd and Sally, left as Cade keyed his mic. "Sheriff Myers here, go Lockhart."

"Sheriff, Miss Smith is on the move. She's on her way to her appointment."

"Lockhart, I told you I was taking her to that appointment."

"I know you did, sir. I'm afraid Miss Smith didn't get that memo." Lockhart's sarcasm wasn't lost on Cade.

"Got it, Lockhart. I'm leaving now. I should arrive only a few minutes after you."

"Ten-four, Sheriff, Lockhart out."

Cade took in Kallie's nervous fidgeting. She looked a little scared too. "Kallie, how can I help? Is something wrong?"

She took a long pause, her eyes watching Cade. They seemed to be giving him a silent message. "Kallie?"

Finally, she shook her head. Her feet started moving backward before she started talking. "No, it was nothing important. I can come back later."

To Cade, her look said otherwise. "Kallie, are you sure?"

She nodded. "You're busy. I can come back."

Cade's brow furrowed. "Kallie, I always have time for you kids."

She kept it moving out the door. Cade followed her out, asking a final time, "You sure I can't help with anything? Can I give you a ride?"

She shook her head, declining the offer of help and the ride, turning to walk down the street at a quick clip.

Frowning, Cade watched her disappear around the corner of the next block. Planning on checking in with her at her home tomorrow, Cade got in his car to meet Mary at her appointment.

∞∞∞

Mary sat on the slightly uncomfortable sofa in Dr. Murrow's office. Lana sat next to her in a chair. Lockhart stood by the door like a sentry. Dr. Murrow was in a deep-cushion chair directly across from Mary.

"We can get started or wait for the Sheriff. Be warned that we won't let the sheriff in the room after the session has begun if we start now.

Mary looked at the watch on her wrist. "I think I'd like to w—"

"He's here." Deputy Lockhart interrupted. He opened the door and let Cade inside.

Closing the door behind him, he nodded at the doctor and Lana, going to sit next to Mary. He took her hand and kissed her cheek. "Sorry, I'm late."

Smiling and feeling loads better, Mary squeezed his hand thankfully. "It's all right. We didn't start yet. I wanted to wait until you were here."

Cade smiled and leaned in and kissed her on the lips, whispering for her ears only. "Remember, always where you are, always."

"Okay, if you're ready, Mary, decide who you'd like in the room. The others will need to step outside."

Mary looked nervously from Cade to Lana and back. "Can't I have both Cade and Lana stay?"

Both showed expressions of relief as Dr. Murrow nodded. "Okay, if that is how you'd like it." He gave a pointed look at Deputy Lockhart.

Shane nodded and said, "I'll be right outside the door."

"Sheriff Myers, I need to ask you to take a different seat, away from Mary." Dr. Murrow turned to include Lana. "And you as well, Miss Miles."

Lana moved her chair to the same side of the room as the doctor but over further. She wasn't as close to them. Mary would physically have to turn her head to see her.

Cade followed Lana after giving Mary a final kiss and saying. "Don't worry. We'll get you through this, sweetheart."

Cade pulled a chair over next to Lana. He was feeling a little tense.

Looking at Cade and Lana, the doctor warned. "I will need complete silence. You two must remain quiet no matter what transpires here. I am Mary's tether to the here and now. She needs to be concentrated on me."

Turning, Dr. Murrow smiled at Mary, ignoring the others in the room. "Now, Mary, I need you to relax, take nice even breaths." The doctor reached over to the coffee table between him and Mary. He flicked a switch on a little miniature ceramic waterfall. A soft light came on, and water began to flow rhythmically. "Breathe nice and slow, in through your nose, out through your mouth. Take a nice deep breath in, slow breath out. Look at the water, feel yourself relaxing. Listen to my voice and relax."

Mary followed the doctor's directions. Cade watched Mary train her eyes on the waterfall, her long lashes a shadow on her cheeks as she looked down. He looked at her chest as she took even breaths. She seemed relaxed to him.

"That's it, Mary, just like that." The doctor's voice lulled Mary further into relaxation.

"Mary?" The doctor questioned softly.

"Yes?" She answered.

"I'd like you to close your eyes now, and let's go back."

Mary's brow furrowed a little. "Back?"

"Yes. Let's go back. Take me back to a time before Eldred before the library. Go back, Mary."

She repeated in a whisper. "Back."

"Yes, that's it. Back, back, back to your life."

Mary softly repeated. "Back, back, back...."

Cade watched Mary sway a little, and then her whole posture changed. She was no longer sitting up straight. Her body bowed into itself; her shoulders hunched; her legs drew closer to her chest. A small whimper escaped her lips.

Dr. Murrow said softly. "Open your eyes."

Mary's eyes sprang open. She looked around her. She drew her legs to her chest, grabbing one of the sofa pillows. She put it on her knees and rested her head on it but first, she popped her thumb in her mouth and sucked as she rocked in agitation.

Watching from his position, Cade was suddenly struck by how young Mary suddenly looked. Her sucking her thumb and rocking enhanced the illusion of her being child-like.

Cade looked at the doctor to see if he noticed. The doctor wrote something down in the journal he had on his lap. After he was done writing, he spoke softly to Mary.

"Mary?"

Mary continued to rock and suck her thumb.

He tried again. "Mary"

Mary looked across at Dr. Murrow. She removed her thumb from her mouth and spoke in a little girl's voice. "Are you talking to me?" She asked and then put her thumb back in her mouth.

"Yes, Mary."

She popped her thumb out of her mouth again. "Not Mary." The thumb went back in her mouth.

Dr. Murrow's brow crinkled in confusion. "Who are you?"

The thumb came out again. "Father calls me Treat."

Dr. Murrow shook his head, his bewilderment deepening. "Your name is Treat?"

The thumb stayed in her mouth, and she shook her head.

"Your name isn't Treat?" Dr. Murrow was trying to pin her down on a name.

Mary took her thumb out of her mouth, pulling the pillow closer to her chest. Sighing and rolling her eyes, she looked at Dr. Murrow. "Father calls me Treat. Father's son calls me 'ceptacle."

Dr. Murrow nodded, although his perplexity was evident on his face.

Cade was beyond perplexed. He'd bet his savings he was seeing a child in place of Mary, the adult woman. The doctor had wanted Mary to go back a year or so. It looked like his session was backfiring on him. Mary evidently went *way* back to when she was a child. Cade wondered how old she was.

Dr. Murrow questioned. "Your father calls you Treat, and your brother calls you Septical? Why?"

"Not my brother," Mary answered in an emphatic voice but still a child's.

"It's your father's son but not your brother?" Dr. Murrow sounded more and more confused.

"Uh-huh," Mary mumbled around her thumb.

"What kind of name is septical?"

Huffing in annoyance, Mary explained, obviously how it must have been explained to her. "It's short for trash 'ceptacle. Father's son said I am a trash 'ceptacle because everyone dumps on me."

A grim expression crossed the doctor's face. "Do you mean trash receptacle?"

Lana gasped in horror. The doctor flashed a censorious glare at Lana. Cade understood Lana's horror. He was feeling pretty horrified himself. However, he understood the doctor too. They needed this session to lead to information on Mary's identity. Cade took Lana's hand and turned his attention back to the doctor and Mary.

"Would it be all right if I called you Treat?" Dr. Murrow asked the younger Mary. Her face crinkled in distaste. Although the person she identified as 'Father' called her Treat, it was blatantly obvious that the younger Mary didn't like the name.

Mary's lip trembled, and her huge brown eyes filled with tears. She asked in a scared little girl's voice. "Am I your Treat now too? Do I have to lick your meat lollipop too?"

Everyone in the room knew what was meant by a meat lollipop. There was no imagination needed. The hand Cade wasn't holding, Lana placed over her mouth so as not to gasp her surprise and disgust again. Cade looked over and watched tears spill from Lana's eyes and over her hand. Cade squeezed her hand in comfort and clenched his jaw so hard he was grinding his teeth. He had to remain seated and quiet. He couldn't do what his instincts were screaming for him to do. He wanted to go to Mary, comfort her, fight her demons. He squeezed Lana's hand again and remained seated.

Dr. Murrow fixed his face, getting rid of his disgusted face. He smiled gently at Mary, the kid. "No, you won't have to ever do that with me." He paused to let the relief flow to Mary's facial expression. She nodded.

Dr. Murrow continued. "I must call you something. May I call you Mary?"

Mary nodded, not removing her thumb from her mouth.

The doctor continued. "Mary? Where are you right now?"

"I'm in my bedroom." She gave a grown-up-looking smirk. "Not the one that I have to sit in and pretend is my room when that lady comes. I mean my real bedroom. Where I sleep."

"Can you describe it to me?"

Mary shrugged, looking around as if she were really in that long ago bedroom. "It's small. And the bed isn't a bed. It's one of those things Father's son called a cot. It folds up."

"What is the other room like that you have to pretend is yours when the lady comes?"

Mary's eyes lit up. "It's so pretty. It's pink and purple and has rainbows across the walls. It has a closet with all the pretty dresses and shoes I have to put on when the lady comes. And it has a little table with chairs and a tea set with a pot, cups, and everything. And dollies that are brown like me and some that are white like Father and his son."

She seemed happy to talk about the room. The doctor continued with the room. "Do you play with the dollies?"

A slight frown showed before she answered. "Father lets me when I've been good on poker night."

"Poker night?"

"Uh-huh?"

"You play poker, Mary?"

"Uh-huh. I'm the poker."

The doctor shook his head in confusion. "Mary, tell me what poker is to you."

"It's when all Father's friends come over to the house and play poker. They take turns poking me." The answer was straightforward and heartbreaking. "I hate poker night. But if I am good and don't cry. I can have some time in the nice bedroom."

Spoken so softly, Cade had to strain to hear the doctor's next question.

"Mary, how old are you?"

Lana again couldn't hold back a shocked intake of breath when Mary held up five fingers on one hand and one finger on the other and stated, "This many."

Dr. Murrow didn't reprimand Lana this time with a look or words. He continued questioning Mary. "Mary, do you know Father's name?"

She shrugged very much like the six-year-old she currently was in her head. "Father."

"Is there anyone else that lives with you beside Father and his son?"

She nodded. "Father's wife." She shook her head and whispered. "I don't get to see her a lot, only when I need a bath after poker night and when she needs to get me ready to talk to the lady in the nice room." Mary looked side to side and whispered even lower. "Father's wife sneaks me food sometimes when she knows I am being punished because I was bad at poker night or I didn't want to lick Father's meat lollipop."

"Are those the only times you've seen Father's wife?"

Mary shook her head. "I saw her when Father's son made me bleed really bad, and he left these marks on me that Father called bruises. Father was furious at his son for leaving 'marks where others can see.'" Again she did that side-to-side look, making sure no one was listening. "Father hit his son until he went to sleep. I saw Father's wife when she came to help me because I was bleeding and couldn't stand up by myself. Father's son hurt between my legs and my back really bad. I couldn't stand for a long, long time. Father's wife took care of me in the nice room. I got to eat good food, not just dog food. And I got to watch the tv that was in the room."

"Mary, will you do something for me?"

From across the room, Cade saw 'little Mary' flinch. He saw it in her eyes. She thought the doctor wanted her to do something she had probably been doing for the animals in Father's poker night.

"W-what do you want me to do?"

"Mary, I need you to take a deep breath and listen to my voice and close your eyes. That's it. Close your eyes and come forward. You're older now. That's it, keep breathing nice and even, nice and slow. Come forward, Mary, you're older. Now open your eyes."

Mary's posture changed. She was no longer huddled. She sat rubbing a hand repeatedly across her nose, sniffing.

"Where are you, Mary?"

"My room." Her voice was deeper sounding but still small.

"How old her you?"

She sniffed and rubbed her hand across her nose again. "I'm nine."

"Is there something wrong with your nose?"

"Father got mad. He hit me. My nose is bleeding."

"Why did Father hit you?"

"He's mad because I am bleeding."

"Because your nose is bleeding?"

"No. Between my legs, I am bleeding. Not like when I sometimes bleed on poker night, and it hurts. Sometimes when they poke me between my legs, it hurts *bad,* and I bleed."

"Father's mad because someone made you bleed?"

"No." She shook her head in confusion. "I don't know why I started bleeding between my legs. It's been a few days since poker night. And Father only made me lick his meat lollipop and swallow that icky stuff that came out. I don't know why I am bleeding. He called one of his poker night friends. He's a doctor. A special doctor. Father's wife called him a gyno... uh, a gyno-something."

"A gynecologist?"

"Yes." Mary nodded. "He's telling Father that it's normal and some girls get theirs early as eight. He keeps saying it's a normal period. But Father doesn't look happy. I am gonna be in trouble when the gyno-guy leaves."

She rubbed her nose and looked to the side as though she were watching something or someone. Which she was, as she relived her, so far, alarming childhood.

"Mary, close your eyes, please." Dr. Murrow rushed to get her out of the place she was reliving. "Take deep breaths, that's it. Go forward again, Mary. Get older, come forward. Now take nice deep breaths. That's it. Listen to my voice. Nice and slow."

Mary swayed a little while her eyes were closed. Her posture changed several times as the doctor's voice put her in a deep trance. Cade and Lana waited on tenterhooks to see where and what age Mary would land.

Chapter 14

"Open your eyes, Mary." Dr. Murrow said.

Instantly Mary opened her eyes, and she hopped up on her feet. She moved from side to side before dropping on the ground and doing impressive pushups. She went from a fairly quick, even pace of standard pushups to Plyo pushups.

Both the doctor's and Lana's eyebrows rose at Mary's display of physical fitness. Cade's eyes narrowed. Her routine was almost professional or regimental.

"Uh, Mary, where are you?"

Mary answered without so much as a pant or a puff. As though she were sitting on a lounger sipping a lemonade. "Barracks."

"You're in the military?"

"Yup." Her answer matched her movements, economical.

She switched from the Plyo pushups to one-handed. She did three on her right hand, then switched to her left, doing three before switching back to her right.

"Where are you stationed, Mary."

"Fort Hood right now. I was in Benning for a bit."

"Mary, how old are you? When did you join the military?'

"I'm twenty-one. I lied about my age and enlisted when I was sixteen. I was found out by the time I finished basic training. I thought they were gonna find out when I took my ASVAB, but Mike helped me get through."

Cade sat forward at the name. Mike is the name Mary had called out for when she had felt threatened.

"Mike?" Dr. Murrow questioned.

"Mike said he'd get me in, and he did. He was the first man to ever keep his word and not be creepy or just plain slime. Mike told me to keep my head down and do good work."

"Mike helps you."

"Mike loves me. I love Mike."

Cade tensed at her succinct statement.

"How did you meet Mike?"

Suddenly, Mary agilely hopped onto her feet. She got in a defensive fighting stance. "These motherfuckers right here. I am sick of these assholes."

"Who are they, Mary?"

"Fuck-boys that can't take no for an answer and don't like a woman beating them on military courses, firing ranges, or even written exams. Just fucktards."

Cade was surprised about her use of foul language. She had been reprimanding him for using foul language practically since the day she left the hospital.

"Okay, Mary, close your eyes." Dr. Murrow stated emphatically.

Instantly her eyes closed.

"Take your seat." Mary followed directions even with her eyes closed and had no problem sitting back on the sofa.

"Mary, I need you to come forward closer to this time. Come forward. Breathe easy, nice and deep. In and out. That's it. Now ease your way to just before coming to Eldred. Come to Eldred Mary. Come closer."

Mary shook her head from side to side. Her eyes closed tighter. Her body moved in agitation. Rocking back and forth, she started a pitiful moaning.

"Mary, hear my voice. I need you to step back from what's happening. You're safe here." Dr. Murrow tried to ease her, but she only became more agitated.

"I-I- have ... to get ... I have to get ..." She shook her head and moved her arms in an almost blocking motion.

"You have to get where Mary?"

"I – I have to get ... I have to get Mandy Odessa! Have to get Cade Myers!"

"Mary, where are you?"

"I have to get ... Sheriff ... and witness. I have to get...."

"Mary, where are you?"

She became even more agitated.

"Mary, where are you?" The doctor persisted.

Abruptly she screamed—a blood-curdling scream.

All three other occupants in the room stood. Deputy Lockhart swung the door open.

Suddenly, Mary was on her feet, and she screamed again.

Dr. Murrow shouted over her screams. "Mary, open your eyes and tell me where you are?"

Cade couldn't take her being tortured any longer. He went to her. Lana followed. Deputy Lockhart moved in also.

The doctor tried again. "Mary, tell me where you are." Then with urgency, the doctor added, "No, don't touch her—" The doctor's warning was too late.

Mary's eyes popped open. "Eldred." She said in a cold tone, answering the doctor's question. Her eyes held a look Cade had never seen before. He raised his hand to calm her. It was a mistake.

Mary blocked his hand and gave him an uppercut to his jaw, followed by three rapid blows to his body: ribs, kidney, and gut. She twisted his arm and threw him over her shoulder. Cade landed hard on the floor.

Deputy Lockhart tried to intervene but was quickly back-fisted, then throat punched, then slammed into a wall all before Cade could even stand. Mary simply went through her paces, eliminating anything she thought was a threat.

Lana's "Mary, it's me, Lana" was met with a spinning back-kick that sent Lana reeling backward into the wall and then the floor.

Cade was back on his feet. He rushed Mary. She was ready. They traded blows and blocks while the doctor tried to bring Mary back.

"Mary, Mary! Hear my voice. I need you to close your eyes!"

Cade caught her foot from a kick she tried to deliver to his chest. With Cade's guiding hand, she landed harmlessly on the floor. She swung her free foot, kicking Cade in his face.

"Everyone, stop moving!" Dr. Murrow shouted. "Mary, close your eyes!"

Instantly she closed her eyes from her sprawled position on the floor.

Breathing heavily, she froze in place.

Dr. Murrow pushed forward his advantage. "Mary, breathe nice and slow, that's it. In through your nose, out through your mouth. Nice and easy breaths."

Dr. Murrow took a look at the others. Lana was just getting off the floor. Her nose was bleeding, and tears streamed down her face. Deputy Lockhart was bent at the knees, one hand against his stomach, another massaging his throat. Cade seemed okay except for his expression as he looked in shock at Mary on the floor.

∞∞∞

Mary sat silently in Cade's SUV as he drove her home. Lana was in Mary's car, following behind them. Deputy Lockhart was behind Lana.

"What happened?" Mary asked for the millionth time since she 'woke' up in Dr. Murrow's office with her friends, the deputy, and the doctor standing all around her, looking at her as though they had no idea who she was or never seen her before in their lives.

Cade spared her a few seconds glance before returning his eyes back to the road ahead. "Do you remember anything?"

"No. No memories from before Eldred, and I don't remember what happened after Dr. Murrow told me to look at the little waterfall."

Cade continued to drive in silence, debating whether to tell Mary what had happened in the doctor's office. Dr. Murrow had made sure that Mary wouldn't remember her session with him, stating that all the information learned could be too much for a fragile memory. Although they had learned some horrible truths about Mary, they still didn't know her true identity. And from some of the truly repugnant things he heard, they needed to know who Mary was sooner rather than later.

Cade hoped to hell that 'Father' character was taken care of by the Mike Mary said she loved. Those words had twisted Cade's gut just as much as the realization that Mary was extremely sexually abused as a child.

Cade couldn't bring himself to tell Mary what they had learned about her. He agreed with the doctor. Mary knowing she was repeatedly molested and raped as a child might put her in a worse situation than she already was. She was handling being without memories. Cade wasn't sure she could take knowing the truth about her past. Like Dr. Murrow said when Cade had insisted she be told what happened in the session.

 'Sheriff Myers, there is a reason Mary has forgotten her past. She doesn't want it to be her past. Being far removed from those criminal acts against her has helped her heal and be a productive member of society. We can not take that progress from her until her mind is ready. And trust me, when her mind is ready, she will remember.'

Cade agreed and remained silent. He would do whatever necessary to protect Mary. Even if that meant protecting her from her own mind.

"Why are you all so disheveled and hurt? Lana's lip and nose are busted. Deputy Lockhart is all red in the face and was holding his throat. You have a bruise on your cheekbone. What'd I miss?"

Again Cade gave her one of those assessing looks. Mary squirmed uncomfortably in her seat, Cade's eyes making her feel like she was a specimen under a microscope.

Cade shook his head. "Let's leave that for now. I have to get back to the station and check out what has happened in my absence. I really didn't have the time to be away."

Mary's spine stiffened. "Well, you could have stayed at work. You're the one who said you wanted to be there for me. I didn't ask you."

Cade's gaze quickly left the road in front of him to look at Mary. Her tone was a lot like the one he heard while she was under hypnosis. He didn't mean to make her feel as though she was not a priority to him. Which couldn't be further from the truth.

He reached over and covered her balled fist on her thigh. He gently squeezed. "Hey, look at me."

He gave a quick glance at the road before returning his gaze back to her. "Remember, always where you are, always."

Mary took in his tender look. He hadn't been upset with her.

"Cade, what happened?"

Giving her hand one last squeeze, he put his hand back on the wheel and his attention to the road. "If and when you need to know, I promise, I will tell you. Okay? For now, I need you to trust me. You do trust me, don't you?"

He glanced at her again, wanting to see her face when she answered.

With barely any hesitation, she answered, "Yes, of course, I trust you."

Cade winked at her and smile. "That's my girl."

∞ ∞ ∞

Mary watched Lana as she said her goodbye near the door, wanting to leave with Cade. She wouldn't meet Mary's eyes.

"See you tomorrow?" Mary asked.

Lana looked Mary's way without eye contact and answered in a voice Mary never heard her friend use before. "Uh, I don't know. I might have a date with Stan Horiwitz."

"Oh, when did that happen? You didn't tell me."

"Uh, when we were at the hospital. I'll call you." Lana moved closer to Cade.

Cade had already kissed her goodbye, a lukewarm one Mary had never received from him before. He had been on his way out the door when Lana had asked him to wait for her so she could walk out with him.

"I am leaving Deputy Lockhart here until Deputy Boyd gets here to relieve him. I will try and make it back before you go to bed. But it doesn't look like I will make it."

Mary nodded her understanding. Whatever had happened at the doctor's office was causing her friends to act differently towards her. Mary didn't like it. But there was nothing she could do about it other than agree and nod.

"Okay. I guess I'll see you guys when I see you."

∞∞∞

"What are we doing here?" Kallie urgently whispered to Casey.

"Ssh, do you want him to hear us?"

Kallie swatted at the bug near her face. "I don't think he can hear us from way out here. I am getting eating alive by mosquitoes." She slapped the side of her face and shuffled from one foot to another.

"I hate to break it to you, but the mosquito season is over. Those are deep woods bugs you're slapping at so vigorously." Casey was amused as he continued to stare at the red barn.

To keep herself from screaming at the creepy crawlies that were possibly making a home on her face, she asked Casey another question. "Why do you keep staring at that stupid barn like you can see through walls or something?"

Casey sighed and looked at Kallie through the darkness. "Aren't you a little bit curious about what he's doing in there?"

Kallie very enthusiastically shook her head. "No. No, I am not." She slapped at her hair, feeling something crawling. "When I called you to let you know I saw the *killer* and got a description of his car, I didn't think you'd have the bright idea of looking around town for him. *And* I really didn't think we'd actually find the *killer* still in town."

Casey looked at her like she won a prize. "See, that's just it!"

Kallie slapped at the side of her neck, not sure she wasn't imaging the crawling sensation or if there really were insects making her a feast. "No, I don't see. I am itchy and want to go home to my shower." She slapped at her right wrist. "Better yet, I want to go to Sheriff Myers."

"No! You promised to give me time, Kallie." Casey implored.

"I said I'd give you time to tell your brother. Not play junior detective in the woods." She slapped hard at her left cheek.

Sighing, Casey put an arm around her. "I'm sorry, Kallie. It's just, this guy—"

"Killer." Kallie interrupted with emphasis.

Casey nodded. "Okay, this killer should have been long gone. Why is he still here? What's he doing in that barn?"

Kallie sighed and slapped at her wrist again. "Whatever it is, it's nothing good."

Casey took pity on Kallie. He gave Kallie a sideways hug. "I'm sorry. The bugs are attracted to your perfume."

"Well, I wore it for *you*. Not them."

Casey kissed the side of her face. "Well, I appreciate it. Let's just see where this killer is headed, then we'll go tell my brother first, and then we'll all go to Sheriff Myers." He placed another tender kiss at her temple. "Deal?"

Kallie looked at her boyfriend. Casey was a good guy. She wanted to remain his girlfriend. "Okay, deal."

He gave her one last kiss before putting his attention back on the barn wall where the killer had disappeared inside to do only God knew what.

∞∞∞∞

Cade sat in his office, frustrated beyond belief. He slammed down the case file, feeling a little defeated. He had gone over every single paper generated by Mary's case. When seeking her identity, he had sent requests with her prints, pictures, and DNA to various databases. In the many databases he sent requests, several were military databases.

So, why didn't Mary's information pop in those databases? She said she had been stationed at Forts Hood and Benning. Her records should have been revealed with his requests.

Cade turned off the light and put his feet up on his desk. He needed a minute of quiet. Although the station was silent, his mind was not. Cade replayed Mary's session with Dr. Murrow over and over again in his mind. The unspeakable events in her childhood broke his heart. Unfortunately, he could easily picture the scared little girl Mary must have been. Her face and mannerism were very much that of a child during her session.

He had gone from blinding fury directed at her abusers to completely heartbroken and sad for the loss of childhood. How had little Mary survived such awful beginnings? However, she did it. She was much stronger than he ever imagined her to be.

He heard the low murmur of the night dispatcher. He didn't even try to listen to the details of the call. He was bone-weary. He'd let Deputy Boyd handle it with the borrowed troopers. Lockhart had gone to get some much-needed rest. One of the troopers was watching Mary's place. This brought his thoughts around to Deputy Struthers. Where in the hell was he? Lockhart had said the last thing he remembered Struthers mentioning was the missing elementary teacher, Mandy Odessa. And now Struthers was missing. At this point, all Cade could conclude is that somehow Struthers had an idea of what may have happened to Mandy, and he went to investigate and had run into the same problem as Mandy. Cade prayed they were okay and together.

This train of thought, of course, led to Mandy Odessa's best friend at the school, Lana Miles. Lana had truly been shaken after Mary's session. The busted lip and nose went a long way in shaking her up and treating Mary differently.

Cade sighed. He was falling in love with a woman he didn't know. *Oh, who the hell was he kidding?* He was already in love with a woman he didn't know and was much more than she seemed. The woman who had been stealing his heart, little by little, this past year was sweet, kind, nurturing, compassionate, and passionate.

Thinking of their lovemaking, Cade groaned. Whether she knew it or not, Mary was an incredible lover. She gave and was willing to receive so passionately. Her body was lovingly accepting and excitingly responsive. Cade loved how his touch seemed to light her body on fire, making his body respond in like manner. An ache right in the center of his chest pained him when he thought about Mary being married or belonging to another man. She couldn't belong with someone else and give herself so wholly to him. Cade refused to believe fate was that cruel.

Overall, the woman he had known for the past year didn't resemble, even a little bit, the woman he had tussled with in Dr. Murrow's office. *That* woman had nearly kicked his ass. He had been so surprised by her agility and abilities. The woman revealed in Dr. Murrow's office was dangerous. It explained something that had always bothered Cade about Mary. For him, the most significant inconsistency in Mary's case, from day one, had been why anyone would want to hurt someone as sweet and kind as Mary. And how did such a nice woman come in contact with an obvious criminal? He hadn't been able to picture sweet, lovable Mary in any scenario that would result in her being beaten and left for dead on the side of a road. However, the woman who nearly handed him his ass before he collected himself, that woman, he could definitely see being in trouble and around criminals or even be one herself.

There was a light rap on his door. Silently sighing, he took his feet down off the desk and turned on the light. "What's up, Lou?" Cade asked one of the sheriff's office night dispatchers.

"Sorry, Sheriff. But you did say you wanted to know immediately when Mr. Somerville woke up. The hospital just called."

Chapter 15

Cade went through the deserted halls of the hospital's ICU ward. The quiet didn't seem restful, perhaps eerier. Ally Martin was at the nurse's station in the ICU ward.

"Hey, Ally." Cade greeted her. "You get around, don't you?"

Ally smiled. "I am a floater for the next month or so."

Cade nodded. "I am here to see Tony Somerville."

Ally nodded. "I know. The doctor said you could see him only for a few minutes."

"I'll keep it short. Thanks, Ally."

"No problem. He's in ICU nine."

Cade nodded and made his way to the cubicle with walls made of glass. Inside, Cade watched a shell of the usually animated Tony Somerville lie still. A monitor slowly beeped as another made swishing sounds.

Cade was reluctant to disturb him, but he needed any information Somerville may have about the intruder.

Cade touched Somerville's hand and spoke softly. "Tony. Tony, can you hear me? It's Sheriff Myers."

Slowly Tony's eyelashes fluttered and then opened. He gave Cade a direct stare above his oxygen mask. One of the machines attached to Tony Somerville began to beep louder. He made a weak gesture with his hand. He was hampered by the I.V. in his arm and another in his hand near his wrist.

Cade patted his hand in reassurance. "Calm down, Tony. You're safe. The doctors say it looks good. You have to rest, though. I just need to know if you saw anything that might help me identify your assailant."

His hand moved in agitation. He was reaching for something on his bed that looked like a tablet with giant letters and the words yes and no. His unincumbered hand tapped at it.

Cade realized it was near his hand because they had been using it to communicate with him. Cade picked it up, positioning it so that Somerville could see the letters and tap them easily.

Tony haltingly tapped out W-a-n-t.

"Want?" Cade questioned. Then it clicked what Tony was trying to say. "The intruder wanted something?"

Tony shakily touched the word 'yes' on the tablet.

"Do you know what he wanted?"

With his hand trembling hard, Tony spelled out H-e-r.

Cade questioned, "Her?" Then, "The intruder was looking for someone? A woman?"

Tony weakly nodded and tapped the yes.

"Who, Tony? Who did he want?"

Fading fast, Tony shook his head in the negative and laid his hand on the no. His hand remained on the no as his eyes closed, and he became still once more.

Cade slipped the tablet away from underneath Tony's hand, placing it nearby on his bed.

Cade left the ICU ward, going over what Tony had revealed. The intruder had wanted information from him on the whereabouts of a woman. And Cade thought he knew who that woman might be. Mary wasn't the only one who lived in one of Tony's properties. Mandy also rented one of Tony's properties.

Cade thought he knew the identity of the intruder. He was willing to bet Never-Miss was here in his town, causing all this trouble. Morrison had said Never-Miss had tried to get Mandy Odessa twice before, and Eldred was her third location. The court case Mandy was set to testify in was coming up soon. That is why the infamous hitman resurfaced. He wanted to finish the job he started. He was here in Eldred to kill Mandy Odessa.

A new urgency went through Cade as he made a different plan to find Mandy Odessa.

∞∞∞∞

Mary rolled over in bed, looking at the empty side of her bed. He hadn't come over to hold her and sleep with her. She tried to not let that fact ruin her morning. Sighing, she got up and took a shower, then headed to the kitchen for some coffee before work.

As she set her single cup maker on, her doorbell rang. Instantly butterflies gathered in her stomach, thinking Cade was at the door. However, on the way to the door, she realized it couldn't be him. She had given him a key.

She smiled as she opened the door. She tried to keep the smile in place as she looked at Matt Madson. He had two to-go coffees, one in each hand. He held them aloft.

"Morning. I bought you your morning coffee you like so much." He extended a cup to her.

Trying not to feel annoyed and not let her disappointment show, Mary took the offered cup. "Morning, Matt. What brings you by?"

Mary didn't invite him in. She remained in the open doorway. She eyed Matt expectantly.

Matt looked over her shoulder, trying to see inside beyond her foyer.

Mary's eyebrows climbed to her bangs. "What's up?"

Matt's eyes returned to Mary's. He was now looking her up and down. "Is he hiding behind you? He can't face me like a man?"

Mary's eyes went wide. "To whom are you referring?"

"Oh, come on, Mary, you know I mean Myers. He's brave enough to sleep in your bed but not brave enough to face me at the door?"

Mary's annoyance got knocked up a few levels at Matt's tone. Her whole stance and demeanor changed in a split second. She stood straighter, and her eyes narrowed on him.

"Uh, Miss Smith, are you all right?" Trooper Ryan Daniels asked. He had seen her facial features drastically change from his position at the bottom of the steps to her porch. He didn't know what her visitor had said to her. But he wasn't going to wait around for the situation to escalate. Her expression was speaking volumes.

The man on her porch gave Trooper Daniels a perturbed glare over his shoulder. "Everything is fine. Why don't you go back to sitting and doing nothing."

Trooper Daniels smirked and got on the porch, standing directly behind Miss Smith's visitor. He knew how to handle 'tough guys.' He didn't say anything, only watched Mary to see what his next move should be. Daniels had no problem throwing the pompous ass off the porch and escort him back to his car.

Daniels stopped him from going to the door when the man had first driven up, asking what his business was with Miss Smith. The man had answered he was a close friend. He had put emphasis on the word close. Daniels hadn't overthought that, although his colleague, Trooper Phil Canton, had told him that the Smith woman was the Sheriff's woman.

Now seeing Mary Smith's face that had gone from sweetly smiling to disappointed to outright hostility, Trooper Daniels believed Mary Smith was about to let her visitor know that he wasn't that *close* of a friend.

She started with a low tone. "*If* Cade were here, it would definitely not be any of your business."

"Of course, it's my business. You and I are the only blacks that are local and young enough to date each other. We should be dating. We should be a couple. It's more natural." Her visitor continued as though he too couldn't see the anger banked in her eyes. "What do you see in him anyway? He doesn't have anything I don't. You know deep down that we are a better match and should be together more than you and him."

Trooper Daniels simply quirked a curious brow, waiting and wondering how Miss Smith would respond. He didn't have to wait long.

With her eyes hooded with anger, she said. "First, your whole blacks belong with blacks crap is just that, crap. I don't believe in any such thing. People are people. They're going to like and love whoever they like and love. For some people, they don't have a choice in who that someone is going to be. Second, Cade has a lot over you in my book, but the one that supersedes them all is he doesn't believe people should be together just because they're of the same race. In my book, that beats anything you have to offer, hands down. Even if this weren't true, I could go even simpler. Cade does it for me. His kisses curl my toes. He makes my nipples hard, makes my panties wets, makes me come like crazy."

Trooper Daniels held in his laugh and would have paid good money to see the dude's face right about now.

When he remained speechless, Mary added, "Now, unless you want to hear more of what you don't have compared to Cade, I suggest you get off my porch."

Trooper Daniels stepped from behind the still silent man, moving to the side so he could see the fireman's expression. Madson was seething with fury. His expression was tense enough that Trooper Daniels thought it prudent to step in front of Mary.

"Okay, sir. You heard the lady. Time to go."

Madson switched his gaze to Trooper Daniels. "I am talking to the lady. You're here to babysit, not listen to private conversations."

Trooper Daniels put his arm out and stepped forward so that there was no choice for Madson but to step back or bump him. "Your conversation is done. I won't be so nice if I have to ask you again."

The fury exploded behind his eyes. Daniels readied his opposition stance as he grabbed the fireman's arm in a tight grip and turned him, leading him off the porch and escorting him to his car.

Trooper Daniels smiled, saying, "You have a nice day, sir."

∞∞∞

Cade knocked on Kallie Kramer's front door. He had spent the couple of hours in his own bed thinking about Mary and the look on Kallie's face when she tried to talk to him. He couldn't forget the genuine fear he had seen. He knew it was early, but he needed to check in with her. He was convinced it was something serious and that she wanted to tell him. For some reason, she had changed her mind at the last second.

Kallie's mother answered the door. "Sheriff Myers? Is that you?"

"Yes, Ma'am, Mrs. Kramer. I am sorry to bother you. I was wondering if I could talk to Kallie for a few minutes."

Mrs. Kramer covered a yawn behind her hand. "Sorry, Sheriff, she slept over at a friend's house last night. I am not expecting her back until after school. Anything wrong? Something I should be worried about?"

"Oh, no, Ma'am. Kallie volunteered for a shift as a dispatcher. I was just stopping by to see if she could do it today after school. I was trying to catch her before she left for the day."

Mrs. Kramer nodded, as it made sense to her since Kallie wanted to major in criminal justice, and she volunteered at the sheriff's station routinely, learning all that she could first hand.

"I'll let her know you stopped by."

"It's okay. I'll catch up with her at the high school." Cade lied smoothly. He didn't want to worry Kallie's mother if there was no need. "Sorry to knock so early."

"That's no problem, Sheriff."

"Thank you. Goodbye. Have a good day, Ma'am."

"Bye. You too, Sheriff."

∞∞∞∞

Billy Tillman sat in shock at his kitchen table, listening to his little brother explain that he was the Red X Prankster that had been causing trouble in town. Not only that, but he had brought his new girlfriend into his schemes. Then to top it all off, while they were participating in his mischief, they happened to witness a murder in the high school. All Billy could do was shake his head in disbelief. He didn't know what he was going to do.

He exploded in anger and disappointment. "God damn it, Casey. I told you to stay out of trouble! What the fuck were you thi—"

Billy stopped talking when he noticed the kids' expressions. Sighing from somewhere deep down in his belly, he asked, "What else aren't you telling me?"

They exchanged guilty and nervous looks, making Billy's temper snap. "What?" He shouted, causing the teens to jump.

Casey's voice was small and frightened, reminding Billy of the night he told them their parents were dead and effectively erasing his anger.

"I'm sorry, Billy. I just wanted to play a few pranks. I didn't know the principal would get hurt."

"Well, he did! You're so lucky there was no permanent damage. And I don't even want to think about all the major damage you could have caused with that power outage stunt. And all the vandalism at the school is going to cost a pretty penny."

Billy's forehead creased with more worry when taking in his brother's guilty and scared face. There was something else bothering him. "What? God damn it! What?"

"We- we saw him. He's still in town. We followed him?"

Confused, he asked, "Who are you talking about?"

Kallie whispered, "The killer." Billy heard as though she screamed it.

"Are you fucking kidding me?" Billy stood up so fast from his chair that it toppled.

"I'm sorry, Billy. How was I supposed to know some guy was gonna get killed when I was pulling my prank?" Casey's eyes filled with tears.

Again, his brother's expression hit him right in the heart. "You avoid these situations by being a law-abiding citizen."

Billy ran an agitated hand through his hair. "You kids get your stuff together. We're going to the sheriff's station. Cade has to know about this guy."

Billy left the kitchen, mumbling under his breath something that sounded a lot like 'dumb ass kids.'

Kallie turned to Casey. "He took that better than you thought."

Casey shook his head. "He's just putting it on hold until after we see the Sheriff. He's boiling mad under his calm exterior."

Kallie frowned. "Oh."

Casey tried to dry his tears on the down-low so Kallie couldn't see them. 'Oh,' didn't cover it. He knew he was in big trouble.

∞∞∞∞

Cade was at the head of the table in the conference room at the station. He had called together a task team. He was going into the woods. All the clues for the key missing people in town were pointing towards the hiking trails. He was also thinking about what Mary told him about Mandy being a prolific prepper and outdoorsman. Mandy must have taken to the hills when she was in trouble, hoping to use her homecourt advantage to the maximum degree. Not only was Eldred her home, she knew the woods and trails like the back of her hand. If she was up against a seasoned killer like Cade suspected, those woods and trails were her best chance of evening the odds and surviving.

Cade had explicitly asked for troopers familiar with the trails. And, if not familiar with the trails, they should be better than average hikers. He was glad to see Trooper Phil Canton on board. The others he'd get to know while the search was going on.

"Okay, we will have three teams searching three different trails. We're looking for any sign of recent hikers, campers, or something out of place up there."

"Didn't the state forensic team search the area pretty thoroughly when the John Doe body was found?" Deputy Boyd asked.

"They did do a good search, but they were looking for clues about that specific crime. I am looking for signs of people camping, living out there, or hiding. I am also looking for the two people whose photo I included in the information packet you all have in front of you. One is

Mandy Odessa, an elementary school teacher from right here in Eldred. And two, one of our own, Sheriff's Deputy, Larry Struthers."

"Any ideas why these two are missing?" One of the troopers asked.

"We believe Mandy Odessa was in trouble from a stalker." Cade didn't want to reveal Mandy's Wit-Sec status. "And Deputy Struthers realized where Ms. Odessa ran to hide and went after her."

"So, we're to assume they're together?" The same trooper asked.

"Assume nothing, look hard, and be fast, be aware there is possibly a bad guy out there too. Now, if there is nothing else, I want to get started."

The troopers and deputies all rose and made for the exit. Sally walked in as Cade gathered his folders to leave.

"Sheriff, the Tillman brothers, and Kallie Kramer are here to talk to you."

∞∞∞∞

Mary sat in the parking lot of the elementary school. The bagged lunches she had purchased for her and Lana sat in the passenger seat. Lana hadn't called or text her since her session with Dr. Murrow. Usually, Mary couldn't answer Lana's texts fast enough. So spontaneously, she decided to spend her lunchtime with Lana. She had stopped at Lana's favorite deli on Main street and ordered Lana's favorite sandwich.

Mary had been going through the motions at the circulation desk. She usually was fully engaged with all the patrons. Today her mood was heavy. Her mood was ruined when she awoke to find Cade hadn't come to her house to sleep. And her mood went down from there, worsening with her little confrontation with Matt. It wasn't like her to be so unbending or rude. She had been both with Matt.

Mary was scared that the person she had been a year ago was slowly emerging in bits via strange and very different behavior. And she couldn't say that she liked the person that was emerging. She strained her head, trying to remember her session with Dr. Murrow. No matter how hard she tried, she couldn't remember anything beyond the little waterfall. Rubbing her forehead, Mary picked up the deli bag and went inside to have lunch with Lana and hopefully get some answers.

Chapter 16

Cade sat back in his seat, watching the extremely nervous-looking trio sitting in his visitor's chairs. They were all silent and wouldn't look him directly in the eyes. Something was wrong here. Remembering Kallie's attempt to talk to him and his failed visit to her home, Cade figured he was about to hear what Kallie had already tried to tell him once.

Since none of them seemed capable of starting the conversation, Cade looked at Kallie and asked, "You wanted to speak to me, Kallie? I went to your house, but your mom told me you had slept over at a friend's house."

Kallie turned worried eyes on Cade. "Oh, no! She's gonna freak out all over me."

Cade shook his head. "No, she won't. I said I was looking for you to volunteer here."

She gave a tremendous sigh of relief. "Thank you, Sheriff Myers." After her gratitude, she reverted back to silence.

Cade's eyes scanned the three with a contemplating eye. Casey seemed the most stressed out. He asked. "Is there something I can do for you, Casey? Everything all right?"

With distress, Casey began to speak non-stop. His words running together with no punctuation that Cade could discern.

"I'msorryImtheRedXPranksterIdidn'tmeanforthistohappen HekilledwhilewewatchedKalliewantedtotellyourightawayb utIwasafraidofgoingtojail."

Cade's relaxed posture disappeared. "Whoa? Slow down and repeat that. I think I heard someone got killed, and you're the Red X Prankster?"

Speaking much slower, with tears in his eyes, Casey repeated himself. "I'm sorry. I'm the Red X Prankster. I didn't mean for this to happen. He killed that man while we watched. We were hiding behind the half wall in the office. Kallie wanted to come to you right away. But I was scared. I didn't want to disappoint Billy, and I really didn't want to go to jail."

Cade sat perfectly still for about three seconds before he burst into action. He shouted for Sally, snatching up his phone. He dialed a number and then spoke briskly into the receiver. "Get down here ASAP. I need a sketch done." He hung up without saying goodbye.

"What's up, Sheriff?" Sally asked from the doorway.

Cade stood. "We're going to have someone in the jail today. Contact the judge and see if he can get a bail hearing set for later this afternoon or early evening." He stood in front of Casey, reaching for the cuffs on his belt. "Stand up. Casey Tillman, you're under arrest."

∞∞∞∞

Lana had reluctantly agreed to eat lunch with Mary in the teacher's lounge. She hadn't come right out and said she wasn't going anywhere with Mary, but she had used every excuse not to leave the building.

"How is everything?" Mary asked a silent Lana. Which was unusual. Often, Mary had to tell Lana to stop talking.

"Good," Lana answered without looking at her.

Mary played with her sandwich, not really hungry. She had tried a couple of times to engage Lana in conversation. Thus far, it was a dismal failure. Lana gave her one-word answers while avoiding all eye contact.

"Cade didn't sleep over." Mary's voice was a little shaky. To her, it felt as though she was losing her closest friends. Mandy was missing, Lana was shutting her out, and it looked like Cade got what he wanted from her and was moving on despite the pretty words he had spoken to her.

Lana froze, stopping her restless hands. Now she looked directly at Mary. "He's a busy man."

Mary bit her lip to keep her tears at bay. "Everyone in my life is all of a sudden too busy for me."

Lana's face went through a myriad of expressions, and Mary couldn't place a single emotion before she said hesitatingly. "We're swamped, M-M-Mary."

Mary frowned at the strange hesitation and stutter Lana put on her name. There was something way off about Lana. She had been acting strange ever since her session ended with Dr. Murrow. *What the hell was going on?* Mary was tired of this feeling of uncertainty and blurted her thoughts without preamble. "What the hell is going on with you and Cade? What happened with Dr. Murrow? Why are you guys treating me so awful?" Mary's voice hitched as she asked a final question. "Are we still friends?"

Lana's chin trembled. Mary was shocked as Lana was holding back tears. As she sat and watched her best friend, her pretty gray eyes filled with tears and then spilled, running down her cheeks.

"What the hell, Lana?"

Lana shook her head, putting a hand over her mouth to stifle her cry of anguish. She stood and ran out of the lounge.

Mary watched Lana make her escape, and she felt her own tears sliding down her face.

∞∞∞∞

Cade hadn't waited for the sketch artist to arrive at the station so he could render a sketch based on the description the kids had of the killer. His sense of urgency had ramped up when the kids confessed to witnessing the murder of John Doe at the high school. More now than ever, he was convinced that Mandy had taken off to hide in the one place she had a distinct advantage. It was her only fighting chance against a deadly killer who was pursuing her with one-track intent to kill her.

Cade was dressed in full hiking gear, plus his sheriff's belt with his weapon and accessories. He wore his shield on a tan hiking vest with pockets with extra ammunition and a knife. He also wore his sheriff's hat and shades.

All the search teams met at the red barn. They split the search area into grids and then assigned sections to the individual groups along with sat-phones so they could keep in touch with each team.

Cade headed one team with his volunteers, while Lockhart headed another with his volunteers. Deputy Boyd led the final team with his set of volunteers. Pictures of Mandy Odessa and Sheriff's Deputy Struthers were sent to the hikers' phones.

Cade had left instructions for Sally to send the sketch via text to all their phones as soon as the artist finished.

Cade dismissed everyone to start their hike. He took the trail where the second John Doe body had been found. Using a leisurely but clipped pace, he headed out.

His cellphone vibrated. Taking it out of his pocket, he looked at the screen. He hesitated, staring at Mary's sweet face on the caller-ID. He couldn't say all he needed and wanted to tell her. He wanted to see her face for a lot of it, and he wanted to hold her, comfort her. He would go against Dr. Murrow's medical advice and tell Mary everything that had happened in her session. Then he would tell her how much he loved her and wanted them to get through this thing together.

He said out loud. "Always where you are, always." Then he touched the screen version of her cheek and sent her to voicemail.

∞ ∞ ∞

At the sound of her name, Mary looked up from her work on her desk behind the circulation counter to find Stan Horiwitz smiling at her.

She stood and went to the counter. "Hello, Stan. How can I help you? Tonight is your book club meeting, right?"

"Yes, it is. I don't really need anything. I wanted to invite you out to dinner after book club."

Mary's mouth fell open in surprise. She didn't know what to say to Stan. He had asked her out several times. Matt, too, had shown his interest in her by asking her out several times. Reminded of her confrontation with Matt this very morning, Mary was reluctant to go nuclear on Stan as well. But what more or else could she do? These men weren't taking no for an answer.

Clamping her mouth, Mary wondered if she had this much trouble getting her point across in her past. "Uh, no thanks, Stan."

For an infinitesimal flash, there was something in Stan's eyes that Mary almost caught. In a blink, it was gone. "Come on, you have to eat. Cade will probably still be on the hike."

Mary's forehead was lined with confusion. "Hike?"

Stan nodded. "Yeah. Didn't you hear? Cade caught the Red X Prankster and believes Mandy Odessa is in the woods on one of the trails. He and a search party went up there to find her."

Mary didn't know which hurt more, Cade not telling her he had an idea about where Mandy might possibly be or him sending her to voicemail all day. After Lana left their lunch, she had really needed to hear Cade's sexy baritone in her ear telling her it was all going to be okay. He hadn't answered any of her calls.

Lana had done the same to her all day. It was the main reason she had gone in person on the pretext of having lunch. She had even sent Lana texts, her last one being just a few moments ago. All went unanswered. Mary was hurt, and she wanted her friends back. One of which is now her lover.

Remembering Lana's excuse this morning, she said to Stan, "Don't you have a date with Lana this evening?"

Mary saw the surprise wash over his face and knew that Lana had lied about having a date with Stan so that she could have an excuse not to hang with Mary tonight.

Stan looked at her, stunned. "Not that I am aware. What makes you think that?"

Mary shrugged, not wanting to put Lana on the spot for her little fib. "I'm sorry, I am mistaken. It was someone else."

Stan frowned but nodded. "Well, now that you know I am free, how about dinner?"

Mary shook her head. "I'm really exhausted. I am going to make it an early night. Thank you, though."

He smiled. "Raincheck?"

What was it with guys in Eldred? Sheesh, what did you have to do to get them to understand the word no?" She didn't want to give him false hope. There was not a scenario where she could see herself dating Stan Horiwitz. Or Matt Madson, or Tony Somerville, or any man other than Cade Myers.

Smiling gently, she shook her head. "Stan, I'm sorry, but no." She kept it simply no. She didn't want there to be any way to read anything else into her answer. His smile disappeared. He nodded, giving a slight wave; he stepped away.

Trooper Ryan Daniels stepped up to the counter. "Everything okay?"

Mary nodded reassuringly. "It's all good."

Ryan smiled back at her. "Forgive me for saying, but you're having one hell of a day, aren't you?"

Mary studied his easy smile. He was the only one on her protective detail who actually came inside with her while working. The others had remained outside, thinking her risk inside her job was low.

"Yes, I am. I'll be all right. Thank you for checking."

"Sure thing. No reason to concentrate only on your physical well-being. There is the mental health as well."

Mary actually agreed with him. "Trooper Daniels, you are absolutely right."

"Please, call me Ryan." He gave her a megawatt smile.

Getting back to her desk, she nodded. "Ryan."

Sitting down, she wondered how Cade was doing on his search. She hoped he found Mandy and Deputy Struthers safe and unharmed. She would worry about them all, and the worry would be tenfold, seeing as Cade and Lana wouldn't answer her calls or texts. Mary said a silent prayer for everyone's safety and then concentrated on work.

∞∞∞∞

Cade stopped for a quick sip of his bottled water, placing it back in his backpack. He had definitely picked up someone's trail. But he wasn't sure whose.

His sat-phone rang. Anxious, he quickly pulled it off his belt and answered. "Myers."

He listened to Deputy Boyd tell him they were headed to a different grid and that they hadn't seen anyone or anything so far that indicated someone had been there. They'd do one more grid and head back down because they were going to lose the advantage of daylight soon.

"Okay. Make sure you mark off the grids. We'll meet at the station when we're all done. I have another section of this grid to check out, and I'll have my group head back down too." Cade told Deputy Boyd before hanging up.

He turned towards one of the troopers that were looking over a hillside. Cade walked over to him. "What do you see?"

"I thought I saw something glint off the sun, sir." The trooper was hanging over as far as safety would allow. "Now that the sun is blocked by some clouds, I can't see anything."

Cade went to the edge. It wasn't just a hill; it dropped off into a cliff. Cade took his backpack off his back and inched towards the edge of the hillside. He wouldn't be able to jump down or walk. However, with the rope, he might be able to climb down.

The trooper tied off one end of the rope, securing it to a sturdy tree. Cade threw the other end over the side. Grabbing gloves out of his backpack, he took off his sheriff's hat, leaving it with his backpack. Removing his shades and putting them in one of the vest's pockets, he smoothly found his footing and went over the side.

He found footholds before lowering himself down a couple of feet at a time. He'd stopped and removed a flashlight and wave it in strategic arcs, seeing if his beam could hit whatever it was the trooper had seen up top. He had done this procedure several times and was down about twenty feet when his flashlight's beam glinted off something shiny.

Cade fortified his foothold and slowly turned, looking to where he had seen the flash. He moved his light much slower, his eyes scanning every centimeter. His grip on the flashlight tightened when he saw the glint again. About five more feet down, leaning against a huge boulder, was Deputy Struthers.

Cade could tell the deputy's eyes were closed, and his head was lolled off to the side at a stressed angle. An angle a person would never put their neck in if they were aware. Swearing, Cade jumped the last five feet and rushed over to his deputy.

Cade gave a sigh of relief upon finding a weak pulse at the side of Struthers' throat. Cade tried to rouse him. "Deputy

Struthers? It's Sheriff Cade Myers." He gently shook his shoulder. "Larry, can you hear me? It's Cade."

There was no response. Cade pulled his sat-phone out. He called in an officer down, gave his coordinates to the state Search and Rescue so their helicopter could find them.

Deputy Struthers had rigged some kind of flare system with his flashlight and badge. It was what the trooper had seen and then Cade himself. Cade checked over Struthers' limp body.

Struthers had blood on the front of his uniform shirt. Cade inspected his injury. His jaw clamped, and his frown turned grim. Struthers had a bullet wound. So that left out him being hurt by the elements or a fall. There was a predator out in these woods. The two-legged variety. Damn.

There was no sign of Mandy Odessa. Cade was hoping to find his deputy with her. Cade sent up a quick prayer that Mandy was still holding her own. When he started out, he was hoping to have good news for Mary. That wasn't going to happen now.

While he waited for Search and Rescue, he thought of Mary, realizing he hadn't seen her in over twenty-four hours. He ached to be with her. But what he desired more was to spare Mary any more anguish. He'd do whatever was necessary to keep her happy and safe.

∞ ∞ ∞

Mary turned off the shower in her master bathroom. She had been in the shower for over thirty minutes, letting the hot water soothe her weary body. Her feelings of sadness and hurt weighed down on her. She had called and texted both Cade and Lana several times since she got home from work. Neither had responded.

She dried off and put on a pair of sweatpants and a matching hoodie. She went downstairs to start a late dinner for one. She carried her cellphone with her on the chance that either of the two people she wanted to hear from responded to her many calls and texts.

She stood next to her kitchen island, wondering what she wanted to make for dinner. She hadn't eaten breakfast, thanks to both Cade and Matt ruining her appetite. Cade for not sleeping over and Matt for his backward view of what they should be to one another. She also hadn't eaten lunch because she had been upset that Lana was upset. She knew she had to put something in her stomach. She couldn't have anything but coffee and water all day.

Just as she decided to put a pot on to boil some pasta for her seasoned buttered penne and broccoli dish, the doorbell sounded.

Glancing at her phone, weighing the chances on whether it could be Cade or Lana. Her notifications had been eerily silent.

She opened the door and frowned as her chances of having dinner dropped as she looked at Matt Madson.

∞ ∞ ∞

"What?" Cade shouted.

Sally gave him a bland look and kept silent.

Seeing her look, Cade sighed and apologized. "Look, I am sorry for shouting at you, Sally. It's just I was really relying on that sketch."

"I know, Sheriff. That's why I am gonna pretend like you didn't use that tone with me and tell you when the sketch artist you called didn't show up, I took the liberty of arranging one from the state boys. They're sending a forensic sketch artist tomorrow afternoon."

"Tomorrow?" Cade shouted again, and again, received Sally's disapproving look. "What I mean is, thank you for taking care of that for me, Sally."

She made a disagreeing sound in the back of the throat. "The Tillman boy made bail, and his brother said he'll bring Casey in as soon as the artist arrives."

Disappointedly Cade shook his head. He rubbed the back of his neck, trying to release some of the tension built up there.

Sally tilted her head to the side and studied Cade. "Why don't you go home, shower, shit, and shave. Maybe go see you, Mary."

Cade looked at Sally with narrowed eyes. He should tell the old busy body to mind her damn business but decided that her idea was perfect. "You know what, Sally, I am going to do just that." He leaned over and gave her a peck on the cheek. "Call me if anything else happens."

Sally smiled and nodded. "I'll pass it on to Lou when I leave. Bye."

"Bye, Sally."

Chapter 17

Mary was unsuccessfully trying not to yawn and roll her eyes. She had been listening to Matt drone on about African heritage and how it should be preserved. Mary may not remember her past, but she was pretty sure she didn't hail from Africa any more than Matt Madson had.

"We have to keep our gene pool clear of the impurities of other races."

She'd definitely had heard enough. "Matt, you remind me of someone." She interrupted him softly.

Matt's face broke into a huge smile. "Oh, really, who? I thought you couldn't remember anything?"

"See, it isn't anyone I know personally. There is a part of my condition that both Cade and Lana find fascinating."

"Oh, what part?" Matt frowned. Feeling as though he wasn't effective enough in his point if Mary was mentioning Cade to him.

"Well, it's the damnedest thing. I can't remember a blessed thing of my past, but I know the history I have learned in the past. I know it cold."

Matt was nodding even though he had a baffled expression. "So, who do I remind you of from history?"

Mary deadpanned. "Hitler."

Matt's start of a grin turned quickly into a sneer. He made a grunting sound and swung.

Mary had been completely unprepared for Matt's smack across her face or his immediate attack after.

His slap jerked her head to the side. He roughly grabbed her shoulders. Shaking her hard, he yelled in her face. "Perhaps it's time for you to remember what it's like to be with your own kind."

Matt forced her down on the sofa, getting on top of her, yanking at her hoodie.

Mary was in shock. She still held a hand against her cheek, feeling the burning sting. Her awareness of Matt came crashing back when she felt his hand squeezing her breast.

She struggled, pulling at the hand molesting her. She screamed. Trooper Daniels was outside. He would hear her and come inside and take care of the garbage.

Matt yanked up her hoodie, exposing her breasts. Matt groaned and lowered his mouth to the top of one breast. Mary hadn't put on a bra, thinking she'd eat and head to bed early. She didn't have on any undergarments, and her struggle intensified when he grabbed the top of her sweatpants and yanked, forcing his knee between her thighs.

Mary screamed and struggled harder. Matt lifted and gave her another slap before grabbing a handful of her hair and pulling her neck into a painful arch.

Feeling the wetness of his tongue winding down her throat repulsed Mary. She screamed again. Then screamed, "No, get off me!"

He laughed and said against her throat. "When I'm finished, bitch."

"No, no, no!" Tears streamed down Mary's cheeks. She pushed at Matt's bulk on her, bucking her body, trying to get him off her.

THUNK!

Suddenly Matt's weight changed on her, and his face was mushed against her throat, and his hands stopped moving.

"You're finished now, bitch!" was screamed from above the sofa.

Through her tears, Mary saw Lana holding one of her thick black skillets from her kitchen at the ready in case the one blow wasn't enough.

Feeling Matt's crushing dead weight, Mary knew the one hit was going to be enough. She tried to push him off her. She hysterically screamed, "Get him off, off!"

Lana snatched his collar and helped her dump him on the floor.

With speed, Mary fixed her clothing and got off the sofa, walking around to the back to fall into Lana's arms. She cried hard.

"Ssh, it's okay, honey." Lana soothed, giving her a one-arm hug as she kept the skillet ready in case Matt got up.

Mary couldn't stop her trembling. She bit her lip to gain some control, hugging Lana tight.

"What happened, Mary? Did you guys have a date go wrong?"

That question had Mary pulling back, wiping at her streaming tears. "No! He just showed up, talking about how we should be together, and he just needed a chance to explain his reasons. So I said I'd listen. Then I told him he reminded me of Hitler, and he went nuts." Mary's breath hitched through her explanation.

Lana looked over the sofa to the floor at a 'dozing' Matt. "Wow. I guess he doesn't like being compared to a racist asshole, dictator responsible for the Holocaust."

Mary hiccupped and gave a weak laugh. "I guess not." She wiped at her eyes and took a peek at Matt. "I think he's my stalker."

Lana gave her another quick, tight hug. "Probably. Come on, let's go call your man."

Mary nodded, allowing Lana to guide her towards the kitchen. "You know I am surprised Trooper Daniels didn't come when I screamed. When Matt came this morning, Trooper Daniels got out of the car and stood behind him until he left. He didn't do that this evening when Matt arrived. He stayed in the car."

Lana stopped walking and looked at her. "Mary, the trooper's car is outside, but he isn't in it. At least, he wasn't when I arrived. First, I assumed he was inside, so I was just gonna knock." She paused, tenderly touching Mary's bruised cheek. "Then I heard your screams. I used your hide-a-key and let myself inside. When I saw what was going on, I ran to the kitchen and grabbed this sucker." Lana held up the cast iron skillet.

Mary smiled, hugging Lana again. "I think I love you."

They laughed, then Lana said, "Where do you suppose the trooper is?"

Mary shook her head as they continued into the kitchen. "I know they check the 'perimeter' every twenty minutes or so. Maybe he was checking the backyard."

Mary walked past her kitchen island to the backdoor.

Lana shook her head, placing the skillet down on the island counter. "That doesn't explain why he didn't respond to your screams."

The women froze, their eyes connecting. Mary turned the lock on the backdoor instead of opening it. Lana pulled out her cell. Mary went to stand at her side.

"What the fuck?" Lana was staring at her cellphone, perplexed.

Mary rushed to the phone mounted on the wall. She snatched up the receiver. She knew it was dead before she put it to her ear.

"Thanks for taking care of the nuisance."

At the smooth voice, the women turned simultaneously towards Mary's kitchen doorway.

"You? You're Mary's stalker." Lana said incredulously.

∞∞∞∞

Cade was feeling loads better after his shower, and yes, a shit and a shave too. Now he was starving. He was headed for the Italian place Mary liked so much. He would order her favorites and take them over to her place. They needed to talk. He wanted to tell her what had happened during her session with Dr. Murrow. After that, he'd clear the air and officially stake his claim. He'd lay it all on the line, tell her he was in love with her. He was bone tired and looked forward to a nice dinner, a serious talk, and then perhaps sex and then cuddling with Mary. He'd be okay with no sex too. He just wanted to be with her.

Pulling into the driveway of Cataldo's, Cade thought about Mary's stalker. Cade firmly believed he was one of the men that had asked Mary out. The only problem with that is every single male, young and older, white and black, and other races had asked Mary out for a date. Any number of them could have felt slighted by Mary's rejection.

Cade was sure he could cross off Tony Somerville. He was in the hospital's ICU ward, recovering from his injuries. Parking, Cade decided that he'd do background checks on all Mary's potential suitors in the morning to see if he couldn't cross some more people off the list. He was more than sure most could be crossed off. The guys were mostly lifetime residents. Feeling secure in his plan, he hopped out, smiling and returning the waves of a couple getting in their car.

If he couldn't give her good news about her missing friend, then maybe he could give her some stress relief by telling her how he planned to proceed on her stalker case.

Cade started mentally listing all the crimes he wanted to cross off his list before Thanksgiving. He got the Red X Prankster. He found the missing deputy. Now he just needed to solve the murders of not one but two John Does, the attempted murder of Tony Somerville, and arson. He also needed to find Mandy Odessa and the missing Marshals.

The good news was Cade was sure Mandy was somewhere on those trails in the woods on the mountain. He believed she was still alive and holding her own with a deadly killer at her back. From what Casey Tillman and Kallie Kramer had said, Cade deduced the killer was the infamous hitman known as 'Never-Miss.' The kids said that they followed the killer to the barn, and he got hiking gear there and headed up the trail.

Cade figured, if he caught Never-Miss, the remainder of the unsolved crimes in Eldred would be solved and resolved. He was convinced Never-Miss killed both John Does, attempted to kill Tony Somerville looking for Mandy, who rented one of his properties. What he couldn't figure was why Never-Miss killed the two John Does, other than they got in his way somehow. Either way, if he got Never-Miss, he'd solve the safety issues in his town.

Equipped with Mary's favorite Italian food, Cade set off to her house with excitement. He felt like it had been ages since he'd seen her. He couldn't wait to hold her in his arms and confess his love. The night was ending way better than his morning had started.

∞∞∞

Mary looked at the person in her kitchen doorway. A smile as evil as Satan's grew across the man's face as he stepped inside the kitchen, snatching Lana's arm and pulling her flush against him.

"You really should have gone out with me, Mary."

Eyes round with shock, Mary could only stare at Stan Horiwitz in stunned disbelief. She shook her head, feeling like she was in a nightmare.

"You're the one who has been harassing Mary and put her in the hospital?" Lana asked with just as much surprise as Mary was feeling. Her face was contorted in aggrieved anger. "The nerdy teacher did it?"

Lana pulled at the arm he had around her throat. Stan squeezed her throat, effectively cutting off any more of Lana's words.

With gritty fury, he sputtered. "If it hadn't been for your silly ass, with your stupid crush on me," He punched Lana in the side of the head before continuing, "Mary would have gone out with me."

Mary screamed out. "No! Leave her alone. Let her go."

Lana was a tough one. Even through her pain, she got her disdain across to Stan. "Puhlease! It's not that serious. I crush on every single guy within a fifteen-mile radius monthly, but I never act on it. Mary knows this. I hate to break it to you Stalker-boy, her reasons for saying no to you had nothing to do with me." Lana antagonized him even as she struggled with Stan.

Stan's face turned a bright red as he swung Lana around by the throat to bring her face inches from his. "You liar! You're nothing but a slut. Mary doesn't need whorish friends."

Lana hit and struggled. Mary was so filled with anger that she rushed the struggling couple with as much speed and force as she could muster. It was enough to send them all toppling over onto the floor, still fighting.

Mary tugged at the arm around Lana's throat while slapping at Stan's head. Lana struggled too, holding the arm around her throat with both hands, yanking. The three scrambled around on the floor, fighting for the upper hand.

Mary pulled his hair. He growled in frustration and pain. Suddenly, his other hand rose in the air holding a large hunting knife. Too late, Mary saw the downward arc. Stan's plunged was deep.

Lana and Mary screamed. Then Lana's hands dropped to the side. Stan pulled the knife from Lana's stomach and pushed her off him. He stood while Mary was still in shock and crawled to her friend.

She cried, tears and snot stream down her face as she put her hands over Lana's wound that was pouring blood. "No, no, no, no. L-Lana, please stay with me!"

Ominously, Stan grunted out, "Now it's your turn."

∞∞∞∞

Cade was halfway to Mary's when his cellphone rang. When driving, he paired his phone with his truck. He answered with the hands-free button on his steering wheel.

"Myers, here."

"Sheriff, I need you to come back." Lou, the night dispatcher, said apologetically.

"What's up, Lou? Is it something you can pass on to the Troopers that are on duty?"

"No, sir. It's a Federal Agent from the Marshal Service for you, an Agent Flynn Morrison. And you have an important message from a D.A. in NYC. And I quote, 'Cade, if you don't fucking call me ASAP, I am going to come up there and slap you,' end quote."

Cade silently swore, busting a U-turn. "I'm on my way."

"Thank you, sir. I'll have the agent wait in your office."

"Okay." Cade hung up, feeling like his night was going to hell.

Cade didn't waste time. He hit his lights and siren, making it to the Sheriff's station in record time. Leaving his car running, he went inside and directly to his office, waving at Lou as he passed the dispatcher's section.

A middle-aged man with salt and pepper hair was pacing in his office wearing a suit and tie. Cade walked in speaking, "Hello, Agent Morrison. I am Sheriff Cade Myers."

The man faced Cade, offering his right hand. "Hey Sheriff Myers, call me Flynn, please. It's good to meet you."

Cade shook the agent's hand. "Call me Cade. Nice to meet you too. Sorry, it's for the reason that it is. Marshals going silent can't be good."

Morrison's countenance turned sad and grim. "It's not. But I thank you for finding my men."

Cade was confused. "Uh, I didn't find your Marshals. I went to the hotel room Marshal Duncan said he'd be in and checked it out. There were signs of a fight, but I have no idea who won."

Morrison nodded. "Yes, I got your message. The evidence you sent to your state lab boys flagged Marshal Duncan's file."

Cade was confused. "The only requests I put into the state lab recently were for two John Does. John Doe number one was murdered at the local high school. John Doe number two was found on a hiking trail. They were flagged as restricted 'eyes only'."

"Yes, I know. Marshals Duncan's and Winter's DNA were flagged at your state lab."

Cade's confusion deepened. "I don't understand. I saw both John Does, and neither was Marshal Duncan. One was even black."

Morrison's right eyebrow lifted. "Marshal Duncan is black."

∞∞∞

Mary screamed at the top of her lungs as Stan pulled her by the hair away from Lana. She put her hands just under Stan's fist that had a handful of her hair. She pulled against him to no avail. Covered in Lana's blood, her hands slipped. He dragged her along the floor through the hallway to the stairs.

Mary cried hysterically and screamed as he pulled and thumped her up the stairs. Stopping one time to slam her head against one of the steps. She saw bright lights behind her lids as pain flashed across her skull and pictures played in her mind like a movie.

∞∞∞∞

Cade and Agent Flynn Morrison had compared notes. They surmised that the killer, Never-Miss came to Eldred to stop Mandy from testifying for good. He had already made attempts on Mandy's life at her other two locations the Marshal Service had placed her. Now that her court case was imminent, the killer came to get rid of her once and for all. Mandy somehow caught on and headed to the trails to hide. She had gotten a message to the Marshals and had tried to rendezvous with them, but Never-Miss had killed Marshal Duncan and took his identity. When Mandy either saw Marshal Duncan dead or killed, she knew help from the Marshals was not viable. So, on to her next plan. She had somehow gotten a message to Deputy Struthers, or he figured out where Mandy was hiding and went after her. Each man had encountered Never-Miss and had lost.

Morrison and Cade were going over the grids of the trails left to be searched, making plans to set off early morning to help Mandy and to catch a killer, when Lou came running into his office.

"Sheriff, several reports are coming in of screams at Mary Smith's place, and we can't get the trooper stationed at her house on the radio."

Cade was on the move even before Lou finished speaking.

∞ ∞ ∞ ∞

With the pain came memories. Mary blinked, not seeing what was directly in front of her, seeing random images.

There was an image of her and an unknown man laughing and high-fiving. Then various images of her stabbing people over and over. She stabbed them in their chest and then ran the knife across their throats. Men of all ages and sizes, old and young, fat and skinny, were with her, and then without any provocation, she pulled a knife, plunging it in their hearts and then slitting their throats. Then images of her driving in a downpour. She was fighting someone, another unknown man while trying to drive. The man yanked the steering wheel, sending the car careening off the road through trees. The car swerved again, after a second yank, back on the road before skidding to the other side and coming to rest at a slant, halfway on the road, half in a ditch.

The man snatched a handful of her hair. He chopped a blow to her throat and then repeatedly slammed her head against the steering wheel and dashboard. The next images were of her stumbling alongside a road. She recognized it as the main highway that leads to Eldred. Her head hurt so much that she couldn't see clearly because of the rain and blood running in her eyes. She had walked until she dropped. The next image was of Cade at the hospital asking her question.

Mary's eyes popped open as her head hit another step. She put a foot out against a banister spoke to slow the progress Stan was making up the stairs. She let go of the counter hold she had on her hair, allowing him to pull it. She instead grabbed his ankle and pulled it out from under him. As she hoped, he lost his balance and tumbled down several stairs. Because he hadn't let go of her hair, Mary tumbled too. They flipped over each other thrice and crashed in a heap at the bottom of the stairs.

Mary recovered quicker. She got up and ran for the front door. Stan caught her by her hoodie near the little table in the foyer. He slammed her into the table, bringing her down. He was on top of her in seconds. Straddling her, putting his hands at her throat, he began to squeeze, choking off her breathing. She punched and pulled at his arms and hands.

Just when the blackness started encroaching the edges of her consciousness, Stan was pulled off her. Mary looked up in relief, only to find Matt facing off with Stan. Gasping in gulps of air, she clumsily gained her footing while the two men went at each other as though they were in a deathmatch.

With unbelievable pounding and pain in her head, Mary flung the front door wide and ran down her driveway as fast as her feet would take her. She held her temples as the pain in her head intensified, and images from long ago assailed her mind again. She was crying and running. She couldn't see what was in front of her, only the images. They flooded her inner sight and caused nausea in her belly. She blindly ran on.

∞∞∞

Cade's heart beat hard against his chest as he prayed he got to Mary's in enough time. Lou said he had already dispatched a unit to go check out the situation. Cade was driving at hazardous speeds, overtaking the unit that was the lead. He was already going top speed when his foot floored the accelerator.

His body and reflexes were on high alert. He couldn't distinguish his siren from the others. He ignored the lights and sirens behind and beside him. He kept his focus on going top speed without losing control of his vehicle.

Without warning, Mary appeared in his headlights. Cade had to stomp on the breaks to keep from hitting her. She was just standing in the middle of the road, holding her head in her hands, crying hard. Her clothing and hands were covered in blood. Cade ran to her. Being careful in case she was seriously injured. He gently placed his hands on her upper arms.

Her eyes were closed tight. Her face was ravaged with tears, snot, and blood. Her mouth moved, but no sound came out.

Using a raised voice, Cade called to her. "Mary! Mary! Mary!"

She didn't respond. He shook her a little to get her attention. Her eyes opened but were still unfocused. They rolled back until he saw the whites of her eyes.

She mumbled, "House, Lana, help."

With those three words, she fell into a faint.

Chapter 18

Cade caught Mary up in his arms and shouted for paramedics that had also been dispatched. Laying Mary on the stretcher and then drawing his weapon, he went with Deputies Lockhart and Boyd, descending upon the house in flanking fashion.

They were at the wide-open front door in seconds. Cade took point. While still outside looking in, he could see two people fighting in Mary's entryway. As he took the steps to the porch, he recognized both Matt Madson and Stan Horiwitz.

Cade entered fast, pointing his weapon at the fighting two, he shouted. "Freeze! Both of you fuckers!"

Startled, the combatants froze and looked at Cade. They both seem to consider fighting. Cade saw it in their eyes. But then Lockhart and Boyd stepped forward, putting them both in cuffs.

Cade holstered his weapon as Matt and Stan were escorted out by troopers. He called out. "Lana!"

There was no answer. Cade wave a hand at Lockhart and Boyd. Lockhart took the stairs, and Boyd walked towards the basement. Cade to the hallway, checking the living room and guest bathroom on his way to the kitchen.

In the kitchen, he found a bloody and unconscious Lana. "I need a medic in here!"

∞∞∞

Mary heard muffled voices. The voices became more distinct when she slowly opened her eyes. She saw a white ceiling before her eyes fluttered closed again, and she listened to the voices.

"Sheriff Myers, we are extremely worried about the blows to the head Mary has received of late." One voice said.

Mary thought, yes, Cade. She wanted Cade.

"And because of the details revealed in her session, I am doubly worried." Dr. Murrow said.

What was Dr. Murrow doing here? Wherever here was.

"Listen, I hear you. I want what's best for Mary. She has had some pretty fucked up days these past few months. I won't have anything done against her will."

Cade sounded angry. What was wrong with him? Who was making him angry?

"Nothing will be done against her will, ever. She needs to remain in the hospital so we can monitor her. Perhaps you could persuade her?"

"Doctors, I hear you. You're preaching to the choir here. Like I said, I want what is best for Mary. But I am telling you right now, if she wants out of here and there is nothing physically keeping her here, I am going to do what she wants."

"She can't go home. Isn't her place a locked down crime scene?"

"Yes, it is. I will take Mary wherever she wants to go. I am hoping she accepts the invitation I am going to give her."

Doctors and Cade were talking about keeping her in the hospital. She wouldn't stay if it wasn't physically necessary.

She opened her eyes, groaning at the bright lights. The conversation stopped, and the three men came to the bedside to look at her.

"Mary, it's Cade, honey." Cade put a tender hand on her head just above the bandage on her forehead.

"Cade." She whispered. She didn't think her voice would be so weak sounding.

"Yes, honey."

She continued in a low whisper. "Lana? Trooper Daniels?"

"I'm sorry, sweetheart. We found Trooper Daniels in the backyard. His skull was crushed from repeated blows. Lana is in surgery right now."

Seeing Mary's tears at the news, Dr. Murrow said. "She's young and tough. She'll pull through. Isn't that right, doctor." He looked at the other doctor.

"I can't guarantee anything, of course, but from my point of view, she has a greater chance of survival than not."

Mary would take it. She allowed herself a small sigh of relief and then a moment of sadness for Trooper Daniels. Her attention was switched to Cade when he spoke.

"Honey, can you talk about it? Do you know where you are? What happened?"

Mary looked at all the men watching her closely. "Yes, the hospital." She sighed and went on. "I was at home. I had just gotten out of the shower and was deciding on what to eat when the doorbell rang."

Her eyes went to Cade's, and she added in an even lower whisper. "I was hoping it was you."

Cade smiled at her and took her hand. "I was on my way, baby, with Cataldo's."

She slowly returned his smile. "I love that place."

Cade squeezed her hand. "I know." He softly touched her forehead. "Go on, sweetheart, what happened next?"

"It was Matt Madson. He said he wanted to explain himself better." Mary looked at the doctors and then back at Cade. "He came that morning too. He said I shouldn't be dating you because you're white."

Cade's teeth clenched, the muscles in his jaw rippled. "Yes, he told me the same horseshit."

Mary slowly put her finger across his lips. "Don't cuss."

Laugh lines appeared at the corner of his eyes as he grinned, kissed the finger on his lips, taking that hand in his too. "I will try not to around you. Go on, what next?"

"This morning, he was annoying. I couldn't stand him, and I kinda told him to go away. Then he asked what you have that he didn't, and I told him so in a not so polite way. Then Trooper Daniels escorted him to his car." Mary held tighter to Cade's hands as she continued. "Then this evening, he said he wanted to explain himself. I was feeling guilty about how I spoke to him earlier, so I let him in. He was telling me why we should be dating rather than you and I."

Mary stopped as she looked at the doctors taking in her every word. Mary shyly lowered her voice even more. Cade had to lean towards her to hear.

She continued for Cade's ears only. "I told him he reminded me of Hitler, and then he-he-he..." Mary stuttered and then stopped speaking.

Cade reassured her with a gentle tone. "Baby, it's okay. You're safe now. Finish."

"He just attacked me. I think he was going to r-rape me." Mary's voice was incredulous, like she still didn't believe what happened was real.

Cade closed his eyes in anguish as he asked, "But he didn't? Rape you, I mean."

Mary's eyes closed tightly as she shook her head. "No, Lana hit him with one of my cast iron skillets."

Cade smiled at that. "You and your friend didn't do half bad against those crazy disturbed guys."

Tears came to her eyes, and she shook her head. "It was horrible. We wondered where Trooper Daniels was and why he didn't respond to my screaming. That's when Lana tried to call you with her cell, but something was wrong with it. I ran to the landline in the kitchen. It was dead."

"We found an electronic cellphone disrupter just outside the backdoor and your landline wire cut."

Mary's confusion over their inability to call him cleared as she nodded and continued. "I am not sure what we would have done next. Just then, Stan Horiwitz appeared in my kitchen with this terrifying expression on his face. He said I should have gone out with him and Lana was the reason I turned him down. Lana laughed at him and said it was never gonna happen. I slammed into them, and we all went down. I was trying to get his arm from around her neck. Lana was fighting too. That's when he stabbed her. While I was trying to help Lana—there was so much blood—he grabbed me by the hair and started taking me upstairs."

Mary decided to leave out the disconcerting images that had gone through her mind as she fought off Stan. Besides, she had no idea what they meant or knew any of the people in the images that had flashed through her mind.

"I pulled on his ankle, and he fell down the stairs, taking me with. I got up first and started for the front door, but he stopped me by pushing me into the table in the foyer. He was so quick. He got on top of me and started choking me. Then suddenly I was free, and I could breathe."

"Why?" Cade asked.

In utter wonder, Mary answered. "Believe it or not, Matt got him off me. Then those two started fighting. I got up and ran out the front door. I kept running until I was suddenly staring at headlights."

"Yeah, that was me responding to the calls of screams at your address. I damn near hit you."

Mary gave him a teasing smile. "Gotta love those reflexes, Sheriff."

Cade smiled and winked at her. "Better believe it when it comes to you and your safety."

Dr. Murrow cleared his throat and stepped forward. "Mary, this is Dr. Spencer. He's going to be taking care of you while you're here."

"I am staying? What's wrong with me? I didn't think they did all that much damage."

Cade was back to frowning with a stiff jawline. "Well, your face and body tell a different story. You have bumps, bruises, and scrapes all over you. And your right eye is swollen, your lip is split. There is a huge knot to the front of your forehead, and you have two stitches right smack in the middle of your forehead."

Mary brought a hand up to touch her forehead. She felt the bandage there before Cade retook possession of her hand.

"Don't touch it, honey."

"Other than bumps and bruises and the two stitches, is there anything preventing me from leaving here?" Mary asked, recalling the conversation she awoke to.

All three men exchanged glances. Dr. Spencer spoke first.

"Miss Smith, I can't lie. I am worried about you. Dr. Murrow and the Sheriff tell me you've had more than two strikes to your head for one reason or another, and you've lost consciousness. Even if all your test come back negative, I'd like to keep you for forty-eight hours of observation."

"What test?"

"You've had a cat scan of your head. I am looking for any bleeding on the brain or fractures of the skull."

"Wouldn't I be in great pain? Probably not able to function?"

"Not necessarily." Dr. Spencer clarified. "A blow to the head can take days to manifest into injury."

Cade added his two cents. "I'd really appreciate it if you'd stay. After the forty-eight hours, I will come and take you to my place. You can stay there as long as you like."

Mary's eyes widened, and brows rose. "I can live with you?"

Cade leaned in close and kissed her uninjured cheek. "Remember, 'always where you are, always.'"

Mary smiled and agreed. "I'll stay. But I want to go see Lana as soon as she gets out of surgery and can have visitors."

"Deal." Cade and Dr. Spencer said simultaneously.

∞ ∞ ∞

Cade was working on very little sleep. After staying with Mary until she fell asleep, he went back to the station to finish the plans with Agent Morrison. It was nearly three in the morning by the time they were done. Agent Morrison went to his hotel room, and Cade went to his bed. He slept there for a few hours before heading back to the station to meet up with the search parties and Agent Morrison.

Like the day before, he split the remaining grids between three groups. This time Agent Morrison was with Cade. They searched all morning and afternoon. When the sun began to lower in the sky, Cade called a halt to the search. All he needed was to have one of the volunteers get hurt or burnt out due to exhaustion.

He wanted to stay out and search because he was on someone's trail. He saw the hard-to-detect signs of someone camping and trying to hide the fact. He wasn't sure whom he tracked. There was someone in the woods with him other than the volunteers. He'd pick up their trail again in the morning. He was ready to see Mary.

He had stopped in the hospital right before going to the trails. She was subdued and wanted out of the hospital. However, Cade had managed to get a promise from her to remain at the hospital for the recommended forty-eight hours. He hadn't had enough time alone with her to really speak with her the way he wanted. He wanted to clarify their relationship, get a commitment from her and offer his.

He had decided almost a year ago he wanted to be with Mary regardless of her past. He had waited for her to feel secure in her given identity. The only problem had been almost every bachelor in town had the same idea. He had played the risk of not asking her out until every man in town had asked her out. It had worked for him.

Now that he knew he didn't have any competition for Mary's time and attention, he needed to tell her that she had no competition for his. He didn't let her past worry him.

The name 'Mike' gnawed at him insistently. Cade had decided to treat the situation as though he and the unknown 'Mike' were dating Mary to see which one she preferred. It helped ease his guilt whenever he held, kissed, or made love to her.

Cade could only hope that with her full memories restored that Mary would choose him.

∞∞∞

Mary frowned at Dr. Murrow, trying not to roll her eyes. Except for a few aches and pains, she felt fine. The doctor had been giving her the reason why it was good for her to stay put until the doctors were ready to release her medically.

Mary wasn't one to sit around. She had to be moving. She had already gone to visit Tony Somerville. She had visited Lana twice, at breakfast and lunch. She had taken a circuit around the ward, spoke with some nurses.

Ally Martin was one of them. After ensuring Lana was going to fully recover because Stan's stab hadn't damage anything vital, they had gossiped, and girl-talked. Lana had mentioned again that Ally Martin and Cade dated for a little bit. It ended just before Cade had found Mary on the side of the road.

Mary had become very interested in the nurse. She watched Ally with her coworkers and her patients. She wasn't just a good nurse. She was an exceptional nurse. She treated all the patients with dignity and respect. She gave them all her best smile and showed sympathy and empathy. Mary had walked around the ward watching her closely.

In her conclusion, Ally Martin and she had absolutely nothing in common. Ally was white. Mary was black. Ally was a nurse. Mary was a librarian. Ally was blond and hazel-eyed. Mary had jet black hair and dark brown eyes. Ally was tall and willowy. Mary was of average height with lusher curves.

Mary shook her head, pondering why Cade had dated such vastly different women. When she tired of watching Ally, she walked two more circles around the ward then went back to her room to find Dr. Murrow sitting in one of the chairs by her bed.

Mary pulled her robe tighter around her and sat, greeting the doctor. He had been speaking for the last several minutes about her health in the long run.

She put up a hand in a halting motion. "Okay, doc. I get it. I am staying put."

Dr. Murrow gave her a happy smile. "Great."

She tilted her head to the side, her scrutiny on the doctor's almost nervous movement. She asked, "Dr. Murrow, is there something else you wanted besides getting me to stay for the full forty-eight hours?"

He gave a fake laugh, his eyes skittering away from hers and returning to look at her shoulder rather than directly in her eyes. "I was wondering if you remembered anything."

Mary held her tongue. She didn't want to tell the doctor of all the murders and mayhem in her head. They didn't seem real. Even though it was her killing those men, it didn't feel real. It didn't feel like her. Until she could come to grips with her visions, she'd keep them to herself.

Without a shred of guilt, she looked Dr. Murrow directly in the eyes and said, "No. Not a thing."

Dr. Murrow's eyes narrowed. He was now giving her assessing looks.

Did he doubt her? Mary hoped not. She gave him a convincing smile and changed the subject.

"I asked Lana and Cade what happened in my session, and they're both closed mouth about it. So, I'll ask you, what happened?"

The doctor nodded as though he figured something out and said, "Don't worry, Mary. You'll remember when you need to. It will come in indecipherable pieces. Then longer, more sensible memories will form more solidly. They'll most likely be chronological. It will start out slow, and then more and more will be revealed as you accept the memories as fact. It will go on until you know exactly who you are and where you belong."

Mary nodded. She was already experiencing the disjointed pieces of memories that didn't make any sense or tell her anything about herself. They only succeeded in terrifying her. She didn't recognize the faces or places in her visions. The images had no context. They could have been random pictures in a stranger's photo album, and she'd have had the same reaction and received the same information, which was nothing.

Dr. Murrow stayed long enough to have Mary recount her encounter with her stalker and Matt Madson. It still blew her mind that the friendly English teacher was the menacing stalker that had given her nightmares, scared the daylights out of her in the library and in her pantry. She told the doctor she was fine and dealing with her emotions. After giving her one more warning to heed medical advice, he left and set an appointment for her in his office a week from today.

Her dinner tray came and went without her touching it. The food in the hospital left a lot to be desired. She walked to the cafeteria and bought a sandwich. When Cade had visited her in the ungodly hour of daybreak, he brought the clothes and toiletries from her home she had requested and her purse.

Now she finished her sandwich then laid back, flicking channels. She wondered if Cade would visit her tonight. Feeling exhausted, she closed her eyes and dozed off.

"You know who you are!"

"Who are you?"

Mary shook her head from side to side. She was mumbling a phrase over and over. A man yelled into her face.

"Who are you?"

"You know who you are!"

"Who are you?"

Mary cried out, turning her face away from the unknown man. He wouldn't allow her to evade his stern face. He slapped his hands together harshly in her face and shouted.

"Who are you?"

"You know who you are?"

"No, no! Please, no!" Mary begged as she tried again to look away, closing her eyes.

The man wouldn't allow it. He roughly gripped her chin, forcing her to look at him.

He shouted again. "Who are you?"

"No, please, no more. No."

"You know who you are! Who are you?"

"Mary!"

"No, please, no more."

"Mary!"

She was being shaken. Strong hands were on her shoulders, shaking her. She moved against the hands. "No! Please no."

"Mary! It's Cade. Wake up, sweetheart."

At these words, Mary fought the darkness and dizziness, moving towards Cade's voice. She opened her eyes.

Cade's face was mere inches from hers. His gorgeous blue eyes held worry for her. He continued to hold her just inches from his face. His eyes scanned her face, looking for what, she had no idea.

After an awkwardly strange moment of staring at each other, he eased her back against the pillows. He continued to watch her. When she asked for a drink, he poured her some water from the pitcher on her bedside table.

She sipped at it slowly. Her throat was sore. She wasn't sure how long she'd been talking in her sleep. Sitting up, she handed Cade the cup. He placed it on the table and looked at her in question.

She stared back, asking, "What?"

Cade gave her a look that she pretty much read as 'duh.' "Are you going to tell me what that was about?"

She shrugged, avoiding Cade's eyes. "Nothing important or that I remember with any real clarity. Just a dream I can't remember."

"Uh, huh." His tone implied the word 'bullshit.'

Mary was irritated now. "What?"

"You were saying 'no, please, no more.' That sounds important to me."

"It isn't. How was the search?" Mary made it clear she was done talking about that subject.

Cade's eyes narrowed, but he allowed the conversation to change because she was in a hospital bed and had gone through a terrible ordeal. He shook his head. "We didn't find anyone."

There was something, though. She could see it in his eyes. She prompted, "But?"

"I think I've found the trail that Mandy is hiding on or around. I can tell someone else is tracking her too."

"The killer?"

Yes. Cade thought, but he wouldn't tell Mary that he thought a very deadly man was on her friend's tail. "We can't be sure."

Mary nodded, knowing what he was doing. "Are you guys going back tomorrow?"

"Not all of us. Hiking could get hazardous for the less skilled. There is a dangerous storm headed our way. The weather service center has been giving us warnings all day. The snow is supposed to start late tomorrow and continue for several days. They're talking over three feet of snow and a history-making blizzard."

"A whiteout?" Mary asked.

"Yes, a bad one."

"Cade, you have to find her. Mandy Odessa is one of the sweetest people ever. We can't let her die up there on that trail all alone and scared."

He sat on the side of the bed and took her in his arms. "I promise, I'll get her down from there."

She pulled back and looked into his eyes. "You promise?"

Cade saw her surprise. He made a fist and stuck out his pinky finger, creating a hook. "Come on, give me your pinky."

She shook her head in confusion. "What?"

He picked up her hand and showed her how to hook her pinky onto his. With their pinkies joined, he said, "I promise." Then he kissed the side of his fist.

She smiled, liking the gesture. "Do you pinky promise often?"

With a serious expression, he explained, "I've only ever given a pinky promise to my brother, Cord. And I've never broken one."

Mary hugged him. With her head against his chest, she said, "You don't have to stay here. I know you must be tired from all that hiking today."

"I don't mind. I thought of you all day, wanting you in my arms." He kissed the top of her head.

She hugged him tightly. "Seriously, I am okay. You should go home and get some rest."

He put a finger under her chin, lifting her eyes to meet his. "Remember, always where you are, always."

He kissed her tenderly before holding her until she fell back to sleep.

Chapter 19

"Fuck! Shit!" Cade swore profusely.

"It's early." Agent Morrison said, standing by Cade on the trail.

"By several hours," Cade said, eyeing the snowflakes falling at an alarming rate. "We have to double-time it."

Morrison nodded, hefting his backpack into a better position on his back.

Cade swore again as he picked up speed.

∞∞∞

Mary smiled and thanked the trooper that dropped her off at Cade's home. The trooper checked inside and outside the house before getting back in his car. Mary waved him off as he drove out of Cade's driveway.

Even though her stalker had been caught and was currently residing in the county jail, Cade didn't want her alone when traveling from the hospital to his house. He thought he'd make it back in enough time to pick her up himself.

Mary had known Cade for a while, but she had never been to his place. They had only been dating a few weeks. She put the key Cade had given her to get inside on a hook next to a coatrack near the door.

It was warm. Cade had prepared his home for her. She looked around the contemporary house with three bedrooms and two and a half bathrooms. The living room boasted a modern fireplace set into the wall. It was the electric kind. She walked to the hearth and started the fire. She adjusted the flames to a low setting after making them shoot high. She set the remote back on the mantle.

The living room had expensive-looking black leather furniture. A sofa, loveseat, and a chair circled around an equally expensive coffee table made of silver accents and glass. An area rug of deep browns and tans was underneath it all. It was a very masculine room, as were the other rooms in the house. His kitchen would be a dream to cook in if one were so inclined. He had granite countertops, stainless steel appliances, and amenities. She made her way into the master bedroom. She paused on the threshold.

The bed was amazing. It was bigger than any bed she had ever seen. It was bigger than a king. She wasn't sure of the size, but it could easily hold half a dozen adults with no problems. She smiled. It was made. He was a very neat bachelor. All the other furniture was obviously chosen to accommodate his bed. He had a dresser and one nightstand. A television was on the dresser, dead center. Mary picked up the remote, finding the local weather station. She listened to the broadcaster tell of the worsening storm and how it was bigger than even predicted.

Mary frowned. She hoped Cade and Mandy were okay up in those woods. She was having a memory of Mandy telling her about nooks and crannies up there that people could get lost in and never be found or pitfalls they could fall and die before they're discovered. Mary remembered how she and Lana had jokingly yawned when Mandy wasn't looking. The great detail Mandy knew about the woods, the trails, and hiking had bored Lana and Mary.

Mary now wished she had listened more. She was extremely grateful that Mandy was a prepper with a paranoia streak as long as a mile. It was weird how she had always seemed to think someone was after her. Shrugging, Mary decided Mandy's paranoia may have just saved her life.

Her thoughts returned to Cade as she checked out his master bathroom. The tub was huge. Cade was a big man. His tub would fit two of him. Or him and someone else. Mary took a moment to imagine Cade and her in the tub doing what they had done to each other on Halloween.

Man, time had flown by with all that was going on. Halloween seemed like a lifetime ago rather than a bit short of a month. Thanksgiving was in just a few days.

As she looked through the rest of the house, her interest was piqued by a pantry-like room off the kitchen next to the door to the basement. Mary stepped into the room. Something pulled at her. There was something off about the dimensions of the room. The only thing in the room was a step ladder and a broom, things someone would put in a closet. But it was obviously not a closet.

Mary felt around the almost empty room on some inner instinct, tapping and slapping parts of the walls and pulling on hooks. The third hook she tried to pull shifted and flicked down like a switch as she pulled on it.

She startled when one whole wall slid to the side, disappearing inside the other half of the wall. A room of more enormous proportions was revealed. A light automatically came on.

In awe, Mary stepped into the room. There was a workbench with tools and a toolbox on top of it. Off to the side, a leather chair was positioned in front of a tv. But what really grabbed her attention were the weapons lining one wall. There were handguns, big and small. Other firearms fell into the automatic weapons category. There were two shotguns and a rifle. There were swords too. An ancient-looking one sat upon an ivory display. Mary didn't know how she knew it, but she knew it was a Japanese Katana.

She went to the only cupboard in the hidden room. It wasn't locked. She opened it. Inside was an assortment of weapons and equipment. There were knives of all shapes and sizes. Throwing knives, hunting knives. There were shining throwing stars and switchblades.

Three shallow drawers were embedded in the back of the cupboard. She pulled the first one open. Inside were syringes and needles of all different gauges. Two vials of a transparent liquid sat in a case. Mary took one of the vials out of the case, sniffing it. It didn't have an odor. The vials weren't marked identifying the contents. She replaced the vial and shut the drawer. She checked the other drawer. One had money and identification. The ID was all Cade's. Opening the last drawer, she drew back, gasping. Inside was what looked like explosive materials. C-4 whispered through her mind. Mary was certain she was looking at C-

4. Quickly she closed the drawer. Running out of the room, glancing back to make sure it was in the same state as when she entered. Her heart beat erratically as she stepped out and hastily found the hook. She didn't breathe a sigh of relief until she heard the entrance to the hidden room close with a soft snick.

Mary quickly went back to the master bedroom. Cade had told her to make herself at home. Shaking her head, Mary didn't think that meant for her to go snooping through his private things.

The broadcaster was still pelting out dramatic coverage of the record-breaking storm. She glanced at the screen. One commentator was standing in a full-on blizzard with a mic in his hand, reporting about the local power outages.

Mary went in search of candles and a flashlight just in case Cade's house lost power. Her hunt produced a half dozen six-inch candles and a battery-operated lantern. Setting her findings on the bedside table, she decided to shower and then get some rest. Her head was pounding.

∞∞∞∞

"Cade Myers!"

Cade sighed and turned to face Sally. "Yes, Sally. What can I do for you?"

"God damnit, Cade. For all that is holy and good in the world, can you *please* call that annoying ass New York City D.A.?"

I'll call her when I get home." Cade said and turned to leave.

Sally yelled after him. "I've heard that bullshit before, Cade. Come on, it's obviously urgent, or she wouldn't keep calling my phone."

Cade waved and kept it moving. "I know what she wants. I'll be ready for her damn case."

Sally shouted one last warning. "Just be damn sure you call her tonight!"

Cade didn't respond. He was tired. They had searched as long as the storm had allowed. It was too dangerous up there to be looking for someone. He hoped to hell Mandy Odessa was as good a prepper as Lana and Mary said. She would have to be to make it up there this long. It would be the saddest case of irony he'd ever witnessed if Mandy had survived an assassin's attempt to kill her three times only to succumb to nature's elements.

He was beyond tired. He was looking forward to having some alone time with Mary and sleeping with her in his arms, in his bed, all night long.

He had made sure Agent Morrison made it to his hotel room. The weather center advised only necessary vehicles be out on the streets. Mayor Olly had already put Eldred in a state of emergency status. Only official county and state vehicles were allowed on the road.

Cade got in his still running truck. His phone chimed. He turned up the heat and checked his phone. It was a text from dispatch. It was the sketch of the killer Casey and

Kallie had given the sketch artist. Cade smirked as he recognized the fake Zack Duncan in the rendered likeness. Well, better late than never.

Fake Zack Duncan had probably followed the Marshals directly from their point of origin. This cunning killer knew how to stay undetected. Mandy Odessa's only hope against the ruthless murderer was her knowledge of the trails and, oddly, the raging storm. The blizzard made it harder for Never-Miss to track her.

Cade pulled into his driveway. He smiled, seeing the warm glow of firelight through his windows. Mary.

He couldn't wait to see her. Using his garage door remote, he opened the garage and drove inside. He waited for the garage door to close before exiting his truck.

He went inside the house. He was surprised to find candles lit on the counters. There were two place settings at the kitchen island.

"Welcome home, Sheriff." Her sexy, sultry voice bade him from behind.

He turned to find Mary with her hair down. No librarian bun tonight. She leaned languidly against the entrance. She was wearing one of his dress shirts to one of his suits. It reached to her knees, fitting her like a dress. Only a couple of buttons were closed. There was an enticing V-shape of skin exposed, an alluring sight of cleavage.

Her warm brown eyes took him in from head to toe. Her eyes spoke to him, told him she wanted him. She licked her lips in slow motion.

She opened her mouth and said, "I made your favorites for dinner."

Cade simply stood in his kitchen, wishing this as his life for keeps. Mary living with him and him coming home to her.

"Thank you."

She sauntered over to him. She took the briefcase from his hand and set it on a counter near the interior garage door. She took his hand and lead him out of the kitchen.

At this point, Cade didn't care where she led him. He'd follow her anywhere, to hell and back.

She led him to his bathtub in his master bathroom. She kneeled and unlaced his boots. "Lift." She tapped his left leg.

He complied, and she pulled his boot off. She did the same thing to his right. She stood and then unhooked his sheriff's belt with his weapon. She walked to the long counter that had his and her sinks and put his belt down. She turned back to him. She methodically removed all his clothes. Only saying one-word sentences. "Lift. Up. Down. Bend."

When he was fully naked, she pointed to the tub that had already been prepared. He stepped into water that was the perfect temperature. Cade sighed as he sat back.

She reached over and placed a bath pillow underneath his head. She got on her knees beside the tub and began to wash him. She didn't speak, only tended to him. She massaged his sore muscles while cleaning them, washing away not only the dirt of the day but his frustraftion with all that had happened. Mandy still missing, the Red X Prankster, two dead federal agents, a dead New York State Trooper, a local businessman hospitalized with a gunshot wound, Lana stabbed. The pressures of finding a killer. The loss of a good fireman and an excellent teacher to crimes they committed. Cade let it all leave his mind. He let it go right down the drain with the bathwater.

When she told him to stand, he did, and she dried him off meticulously. Then she took his hand and led him to his bed.

"Lie down." She smiled at him.

Didn't have to tell him twice. He only asked, "Stomach or back?"

"Stomach, first."

Cade laid on his stomach and felt his cock begin to stiffen when she straddled his legs. He heard a snap and looked back at her. She had a bottle of massage oil. She poured some into her hands.

She massaged him, starting with his feet. She didn't miss a single toe, arch, dip, or heel. Her small hands were strong. They massaged all his aches and pains away except the ache in his loins. There, his ache for her grew along with his dick.

Since she kneaded his ass cheeks and lower back, his dick had been getting harder and harder. He was so turned on by the time she said, "Turn over," that when he went on his back, his cock sprang up like a flagpole.

She ignored it and started her massaged with his face. She traced his cheekbone, lip, and brow. Cade moaned and thrust upward. When she straddled him after he flipped over, he felt her pussy against him. She wasn't wearing any panties or bra underneath his shirt. That bit of information drove him nuts.

"Mary, I—"

"Ssh," she placed a finger across his lips.

He relaxed even more into his mattress, allowing her to take control. When she massaged everything but his cock, Cade thought he'd die of frustration when he felt her mouth on the head of his dick. His eyes popped open so he could watch her take his dick in her mouth. Her eyes caught his. She stared at him unblinkingly as she pleasured him, taking him deeply while swiping her tongue along the shaft. She pulled his cock out, so only his head was in her mouth, and she rapidly swirled her tongued around the rim of the head while stroking his shaft.

Cade's toes curled hard, and his body arched. She touched his balls, stroking them while she sucked deep on his cock again, his head hitting the back of her throat.

"Oh, God, baby! That's sooo, sooo good!"

She sucked him hard, deep, and fast. Her head bobbed as fast as his pelvis thrust. A light show played behind his eyes as his balls tightened up, and he shot his load. He expected to feel the cooler air when she pulled back so he could finish coming on his belly and chest or wherever his come went. But Mary kept a perfect seal around his dick, giving him the full treatment by not releasing his dick in mid-ejaculation.

As he calmed down, he felt a sharp sting on his right thigh. He brushed at his thigh, wiping the irritation away. He smiled big and looked at Mary. "That was incredible, Mary." He laughed. "I don't know what I did to deserve that but whatever it was, tell me, so I can do it again. Thank you, sweetheart."

At her silence, he looked closer at her. She was still sitting between his wide-spread legs. She had an odd expression on her face. Cade couldn't place it. He leaned up on his elbows. "What's the matter?"

"You taste different."

He started to laugh, but her expression caused his heart to stop for a single beat before hammering on crazily. "Different than what?"

"Your eyes are kinder. And you're not a liar."

Her voice was different too. It dawned on Cade what it was about her expression. Something was missing from it that was usually there when she was with him. And he knew what wasn't there. Mary's eyes held no recognition or admiration and respect. She looked at him as though she didn't know him.

"Mary, what is it? What's wrong, baby?"

She moved so swiftly Cade didn't have time to react. The knife was in his side before he could blink. She was lying on top of him with her left hand, holding the knife in his right side. Her right hand closed his mouth as she said between gritted teeth. "Don't call me *baby*."

Her face was about three inches above his. She looked down at him. She watched him like a medical examiner looked at a corpse, looking for the cause of death. Her right hand pushed his hair off his forehead as he started to pant.

"Uh, uh. Nice slow breaths, Sheriff Myers. That choppy breathing you're doing will have you bleeding out like a stuck pig."

Merriment danced in her eyes as she laughed and then said. "I guess you are...a stuck pig. Ha, ha, get it? Stuck pig?"

"M-Mary, why?" Cade got out in a whisper after he took her advice and slowed his breathing.

Mary got up. She pulled his shirt over her head. She turned and gave him her ass. Looking over her shoulder, she sassed. "I have a killer ass, don't I?"

Cade's heart broke inside his chest. He didn't know this person. The woman in the room with him right now had taken his Mary away. He tried not to panic as he felt his blood pour out of him. He controlled his breathing. He pulled part of the blanket to put pressure on his wound. He was of a mind to pull the knife out, only it was keeping most of the blood inside his body. He'd bleed faster if he pulled it out. He kept it in his body and positioned the blanket around the knife, putting as much pressure as he could. Surprisingly, his pain wasn't as much as one would expect from a stab wound.

He looked at her getting dressed for the weather outside.

"Why?" He asked again, trying to catch her eyes.

She looked over at him. Tilting her head, she said, "I have to get Mandy Odessa and Sheriff Cade Myers." Her voice sounded like a recording. She sounded like an automaton.

She shook her head as if to clear it. Cade had heard that phrase before. During her session with Dr. Murrow, she had said it when he pulled her memories closer to the time she got hurt. Closer to the time she arrived in Eldred.

Cade would never forget her cold eyes when she had opened them and announced she was in Eldred. Her eyes then lacked sympathy, empathy, compassion, and passion. They were dead eyes.

"You r-recovered your memories," Cade said with a dry mouth. It wasn't a question. It's the only thing that explained her behavior. "Y-You know who you are."

As she put on hiking boots, she smirked at him. "You're a real genius, ain't ya? Hard to believe the NYPD is getting along without you."

"Mary, please, tell me who you are? Consider it a dying w-wish." Cade felt himself slipping, his eyes getting heavy.

Mary walked towards the bed. She observed him through blank and uncaring eyes. "Okay, since you were able to make me come and actually enjoy sex, I'll tell you a few things. I remember the first time some slimy guy put his hands between my legs. I was in pre-k. He rubbed between my legs while he yanked on that thing between his. Then I was put in foster care. Yippie. Right?" She shook her head. "Wrong. That pig raped me the second night I was in his home and then every night after that for the next year or so. Then came his sick son joining in on the 'fun.' Then came poker night."

Cade's tears slipped down his face. "Mary, don't do this. I am not y-your e-enemy."

"You're not a good guy either. I found your little room. That doesn't look like a good guy room to me. It looks like a sick guy's room. Like the scum at poker night. Those sick bastards passed me around like an hors d'oeuvre. Except I was also the main meal. You wouldn't believe the punishment the female body can take and still function." She shrugged and added, "But it makes sense when we think of childbirth."

"Mary, I am so sorry that happened to y-you. But I -I am not a bad guy."

"Sure, you're not. Well, you'll find out soon enough. I injected you with the stuff in one of those vials in your little room if you wondered why you are feeling extra weak right now. If the vial stuff doesn't kill you, you'll bleed out."

"Mary, I-I- love you." Cade wanted her to know that even if he died by her hand.

Her eyes actually showed surprise. Then she busted out laughing. She laughed so hard tears came to her eyes too.

She even slapped her knee. "Wooh, boy, that's a good one."

"T-ruth." He panted.

She paused, looking deeply into his eyes. With half-closed lids, Cade returned her look. For just a second, he saw 'Mary' then she blinked and his Mary was gone.

She leaned over him and kissed him. She leaned back, staring into his eyes for a long moment.

"Mary, answer qu-questions for me?"

She stared at him for several seconds longer. Cade kept his eyes open as best he could.

"Okay. I'll indulge you. What do you want?"

"Why are you leaving? There is a blizzard out there. You could die."

She tilted her head and gazed at him like he was an unknown specimen, something she had never seen before. "That's what you want to know with your dying breath? How I'll weather the storm?"

He gave a slight nod. "I-I love you."

Her brow furrowed, but she answered. "I am equipped to handle the weather. I know what I am doing. I have to get Mandy Odessa."

"Get her? How? She's h-hiding."

"I know where she is. I remember her telling me about this little-known cave up on one of the mountain's north ridge trails. I am pretty sure she is hiding there."

"Kil-Killer up there too."

She smirked. "Don't worry, Sheriff. I'll get that fucking asshole too. I owe him one for nearly killing me over a year ago. Don't worry, you'll be able to clear all the God damn murder cases you have here."

Cade felt himself fading. He had to ask before he ultimately passed out. "Mary, who are you?"

With a slow smile and a quirked brow, she said, "I am Never-Miss."

THE END (of part 1)

Read the exciting conclusion in the Summer of 2021.

PART 2

"Whiteout: The Hunt for Never-Miss"

ABOUT THE AUTHOR

Cate Mckoy is a hybrid of a multi-genre fiction author, screenwriter, and ghostwriter. She has two series of books and several stand-alone novels.

She also has a children's books series, the 'Learn With Me Series.' Cate is often working on several projects at once.

Her current big project is called the 'Triple Play.' She will convert three of her screenplays into three separate novels from three different genres and released them all on the same day.

The TRIPLE PLAY will be released on 12/31/20. She is excited and nervous about this project. She wants to do something no writer has ever done before, and she hopes that she will be successful with this endeavor.

Cate is a mother and nana. She hails from New York and still lives there today with her minor-aged son. She enjoys visits with her adult children when she can. She continues to write and wishes everyone, Happy Reading!

CATE'S SOCIAL MEDIA LINKS

Twitter - www.twitter.com/ckmckoy917

Facebook - www.facebook.com/AuthorCateMckoy

Instagram - www.instagram.com/ckmckoy

Amazon - www.amazon.com/Cate-Mckoy/e/B00JCOJVNC

Pinterest - www.pinterest.com/catemckoy

Author's Pages:

Amazon - www.amazon.com/Cate-Mckoy/e/B00JCOJVNC

Facebook - www.facebook.com/AuthorCateMckoy

Facebook Reader's Group
www.facebook.com/groups/CateMckoyReadersGroup

Contact- ckmckoy@yahoo.com

Made in the USA
Middletown, DE
18 August 2023

36953938R00166